Edgar and Emma

A novel after Jane Austen

Robert Rodi

Book One

✍

CHAPTER ONE

"I cannot imagine," said Sir Godfrey to his lady, "why we continue in such insufficient lodgings as these, in a paltry market-town, while we have three good houses of our own situated in some of the finest parts of England, and perfectly ready to receive us!"

"I'm sure, Sir Godfrey," replied Lady Marlow, "it has been much against my inclination that we have stayed here so long; or why we should ever have come at all indeed, has been to me a wonder, as none of our houses has been in the least want of repair."

"Nay, my dear," answered Sir Godfrey, "you are the last person who ought to be displeased with what was always meant as a compliment to you; for you cannot but be sensible of the very great inconvenience your daughters and I have been put to during the seven months we have remained crowded in these lodgings in order to give you pleasure."

"My dear," replied Lady Marlow, "how can you stand and tell such lies, when you very well know that it was merely to oblige the girls and you, that I left a most commodious house situated in a most delightful country and surrounded by a most agreeable neighborhood, to live cramped up in lodgings on a very close street, in a smoky and unwholesome town, which has given me a continual fever and almost thrown me into a consumption."

This Sir Godfrey could not let pass. He put down his newspaper and looked across the table at his wife, which was not something he did often; so that on this occasion he was momentarily diverted from his impatience by a tremor of surprise at what she looked like—which was, several years older than the last time he had bothered. But this he set aside and in great indignation said, "And what ever did I hear from you, when we were happily housed in the country, but how you missed society, and the theatre, and the shops? So that I was compelled to find us accommodation here in Chipping Norton, where I have presumed you were perfectly contented."

Lady Marlow regarded him with as much surprise as if he had climbed atop the table and mewed like a cat. "What can you mean by such nonsense?" she asked. "We see no one here, for there is no one worth seeing; the shops, while admittedly more numerous, are inferior to those in the country; and never once in seven months have we attended any theatricals. Indeed I am uncertain whether there is a playhouse in town. No, no, husband," she said, setting down the tambour on which she was embroidering a rather exaggerated floral scene, "we came to Chipping Norton solely that you might be closer to your business interests."

Sir Godfrey was all astonishment. He had perhaps forgotten he had any such thing as business interests. "My dear," he said when he had recollected himself, "I employ agents to act on my behalf specifically that I might live far afield from the world of commerce. It is distasteful to me;

surely that much has been made plain to you, over the long span of our marriage."

Lady Marlow was no more accustomed to looking at her husband than he at her, so that it was a surprise to both to be seeing each other, after so many years of wedlock, as if for the first time. Yet each was possessed of a congenial, imperturbable character, and thus found in the discovery of their mutual misunderstanding no cause for vexation or regret. Indeed, once they had concluded that the only persons to benefit from their seven-month sojourn in Chipping Norton were Sir Godfrey's agents, who had needed to travel so much shorter a distance to report their activities to their employer, they could not withhold their laughter.

(At this juncture, my readers may wonder why, if Sir Godfrey had meant to give his wife and daughters the benefit of an urban residence, he had not chosen the capital, far superior to any market-town; but Sir Godfrey would never consider London—not since an incident, some twenty years earlier, involving two ladies and a barouche, that had exposed him to the laughter of nearly all of Kensington Park. It had not been the fault of the two ladies, and Sir Godfrey could have no satisfaction in blaming the horse; so he held the entire city accountable, and refused to dignify it with its presence until it had apologized, which to this date it had not troubled to do.)

"Well," said Sir Godfrey once he had recovered from his attack of mirth, "I see no reason for staying any longer in these narrow rooms than we already have. I will this very day begin arrangements to leave them."

"I will certainly not hinder you," said his wife. "But we ought first to determine where we will go."

"For my part, I would be content with any of our houses," said Sir Godfrey.

"As would I," concurred Lady Marlow.

This was the disadvantage to the agreeability of their characters; it often rendered them helpless in the face of a decision.

"Let us apply to the children," said Lady Marlow at last. "They are far more particular than we."

These children were three in number. Sir Godfrey and Lady Marlow had two grown daughters, Frances and Emma, the former of whom had nineteen years, the latter, eighteen. They also counted as their own a boy, Thomas Peake, who was the son of one of Sir Godfrey's cousins; the Marlows had taken him in after his parents perished at sea. This was not entirely a philanthropic arrangement, for they had assumed the lad would grow up to marry one of their daughters.

But with every passing year it became increasingly evident that Tom was the kind of man who would never marry at all. At twenty he possessed the settled, unvarying qualities of a gentleman thrice his age, and a steadfast disinclination ever to alter them. He had accepted Sir Godfrey's offer to finance his training for the law and had undertaken his studies at Cambridge, so that his immediate future was as thoroughly charted as he could wish it. In the meantime, he made himself valuable to his guardians in an hundred different ways, which ameliorated their disappointment that he would be taking neither of their girls off their hands.

Alas, in the present difficulty he was of no use whatsoever. "I have already prevailed too much on your good natures," he said with genuine humility when asked where he thought the family ought next to move. "And as I am soon to return to university, and will thus spend little time at whichever house is chosen, I feel my own preference—if I had one—which I do not—must be disregarded."

Edgar and Emma

Emma was applied to next. She was very glad to hear that the family was to depart Chipping Norton, as she had not thrived there; she was a delicate creature, and the hustle-and-bustle of the market town's streets buffeted her like a bit of flotsam on a rough sea. She was also afflicted with a short temper, and on those occasions when her treatment at the hands of the town's populace was unusually brusque, she very sharply made her displeasure known; this had not increased her popularity.

She had also liked, in her youth, to respond to disappointment or rebuke by dramatically fleeing upstairs to her bedroom for the rest of her life, a stratagem she employed sometimes as often as twice a season, but to which she could not resort in Chipping Norton because the family lived on a single level, and her bedroom was just off the parlour; which robbed the gesture of much of its flair.

Yet in general she was a sweet girl, and strove to be kind and to be fair. To which end she now gave the question her parents had put to her, her most impartial consideration.

The Marlows' three houses were Graftings in Sussex; Dunfosters in Wiltshire; and Penwether in Cornwall. The latter was the least to be desired, simply due to its distance —its sole appeal being its connection to the family of Lady Marlow, whose grandfather had inherited it from a distant relation.

Dunfosters was a very fine house in very fine neighborhood, situated amidst nearly five-and-twenty families of quality, which made for a rich, invigorating society. Dunfosters was also the house in which the family had spent nearly every Christmas, so that it afforded many happy memories of that kind. And finally, Dunfosters was the house from which they had repaired, seven months before, to their lodgings in Chipping Norton; so a return to its doors would be akin to picking up a thread that had been but momentarily dropped. Their Wiltshire friends and acquaintances were a mere seven months the older, and could be counted on to be still in sympathy and accord with the Marlows' manners, habits, and tastes.

Graftings, by comparison, was a smaller house, located in a village—Marlhurst; and while this village was the family's ancient seat, its society had not much increased over the centuries, so that it was today restricted to a mere thirteen families, and not all of unimpeachable reputation. (One household numbered among its progeny a daughter who had made a profession of singing in Italian; another, a son who had gone to live in Turkey and married a Moslem —some whispered two.) And as the Marlows had not stayed there for nearly five years, most of those families would, encountered anew, be akin to strangers.

In addition, the countryside was the hilliest in all Sussex, which made walking more effortful than Emma generally liked. And the house itself was enclosed by a large copse, which tended to render its rooms chilly even in high summer. Lady Marlow had asked to have the trees cut down, but Sir Godfrey refused her on the principle that they were "fine old yews" and afforded them a cloak of privacy. At which point Emma had suffered one of her fits of temper, and asked for what reason the family of Sir Godfrey Marlow required such concealment, adding that she supposed they were too far inland to make a smuggling operation at all practical.

Sir Godfrey had not appreciated her wit; and the memory of this moment's disgrace, along with all the other inconveniences, ought to have stricken Graftings from consideration. And yet the property boasted one other feature that for Emma overrode all the rest; which was its proximity to Willmot Lodge.

This was a villa on the outskirts of Marlhurst which served as the residence of Mr. Erasmus Willmot, his wife, and their nine children. One might be forgiven for thinking that in so large a family, it would be difficult to distinguish any individual; but for Emma there was one inhabitant of Willmot Lodge who outshone all the others.

Edgar, the eldest son, was seven years her senior, and had been a romantic figure in her impressionable girlhood. This had required a good deal of imagination, for he was a quiet, aloof, serious-minded young man, with dark hair and darker eyes, whose conversation ran from very little to none at all. Indeed there was nothing about him that might charitably be called attractive—especially with a brother, a year younger, who was everything he was not: fair-haired, jovial, and eager to please. Yet Edgar had the aura of The Heir about him; and as his father had a considerable share in a lead mine there was, as sometimes in society there was not, a substantial inheritance for The Heir to be heir to.

This initial fancy might have faded over time, as Emma grew to young womanhood and gained a deeper understanding of the wider world and her family's place in it. But such was not to be. For one day when she was thirteen, she had gone out for a walk—her youthful determination not in the least thwarted by the unruliness of the hills or the briskness of a late October morning—and badly turned her ankle while descending a slope too quickly. Unable to carry herself farther, she sat herself upon a stone and examined her injury, and attempted to gauge whether she risked greater impairment if she forced herself to walk on it, or whether she would be obliged to hop on one foot all the way back to Graftings (which seemed to be an ideal plan for similarly disabling the other ankle).

She was considering this dilemma when a rustling in the fallen leaves very near to her drew her eye; and therein she discovered a long, brown snake.

She screamed; and as if considering that this single emission did insufficient justice to the full horror of her situation, she paused but briefly, then screamed again.

The snake—which was perhaps deaf—did not flee or retreat, or bury itself more deeply in its cover of leaves, but slithered closer to where Emma sat, and coiled itself around her heel.

She was up in a heartbeat and began to run away; but on her second step, when her injured ankle bore the full measure of her weight, she flinched in pain and folded like a cloth doll; and while she managed to hop a few more paces in a blind panic, it was inevitable that her lurching and flailing should end in a fall.

She lay for a moment in the dirt, panting in fear, then propped herself up on her elbow to see whether the murderous viper had given pursuit.

And what she saw instead was Edgar Willmot. He came over the rise, his bearing stately and his manner phlegmatic, accompanied by one of the family's Irish setters, which he then gestured into a sit; upon which command being obeyed he turned to Emma, clicked his heels and tipped his hat, and said, "I heard you cry out. May I be of assistance?"

"Oh, yes, please," Emma burbled. "I've hurt my ankle— I cannot walk—" And at this, Edgar began to approach her, so that she must exclaim, "—Be careful, there is a snake!"

He stopped and cast his gaze at the ground, though appearing to be more curious than fearful.

"I see none," he said calmly.

"It was just there," she whimpered, indicating the stone from which she had recently propelled herself.

Edgar turned his scrutiny in the direction she had indicated. Then a sudden movement galvanized his searching eyes, and he stepped forward very decisively, reached down, and plucked something up.

It was the snake.

Emma could not but feel somewhat foolish on seeing the creature dangle between Edgar's thumb and forefinger, for it was rather slight. It had seemed so much longer when oscillating between the leaves.

"This is a mere grass snake," he explained; "it is not venomous. It poses no threat of any kind, to you or to anybody."

Her face burned, and she felt her angry wit well up. "I daresay I should not be lying here, if that were so."

He took no offense; in fact, he smiled. "It was fear of the creature that harmed you, not the creature itself," he said, and he masterfully flung the thing many yards away.

She lowered her eyes. "How stupid you must think me!"

"Not at all. I can perfectly understand how its discovery must have startled you." He renewed his approach. "I often think there is nothing quite so disconcerting as coming upon life where none is expected." He crouched down next to her. "Several months past I opened a drawer in my room, and reached into it for a pocket handkerchief; but what my hand closed about instead, was a mouse."

"Oh!" Emma squealed. "How dreadful! Were you quite alarmed?"

"No less so than the mouse," he said with a grin. "Although that was considerably. Shall I lift you?"

She felt her face flush. "You needn't put yourself to such trouble; if you but lend me your arm, I can hop alongside you."

"That ill suits your dignity as the daughter of a baronet," he said. And with that, he scooped her into his arms and raised himself to his feet. Emma felt the sensation of the earth moving away from her, and without thinking sought to steady herself by throwing her arms about his neck.

He was unfazed by this sudden intimacy. He quarter-turned his head and said, "Come, Pompey," and his dog happily leapt to his side.

Twelve minutes later—during which not a single word passed between them (she being unwilling to add to his exertions by obliging him to talk)—he delivered her to the front door at Graftings, and into the care of her mother. He tipped his hat again and bade them both good day, before turning and departing, Pompey trotting at his heels.

Since that day, for Emma, there had been no other hero in all of Britain but Edgar Willmot.

Alas, there had been little chance for further encounters between them. Autumn swiftly gave way to winter, and within two months the Marlows relocated to Dunfosters for Christmas; and at Dunfosters they remained for four additional years, until they moved to Chipping Norton.

There was nothing in the world that Emma wished more dearly than to return to Marlhurst, and to see Edgar Willmot once more. She wondered what changes five years might have wrought in him; he would now be twenty-five! A vast age. But no change in him could compare with the alteration in her; for she had been a mere child when last they met. Now she was a grown woman of eighteen; would he even know her? Would he *care* to know her? She yearned to find out.

Edgar and Emma

And yet she was a conscientious girl, and meant to do her duty by her father and mother; and it was so seldom that they asked her opinion on anything, she felt she must honor their request by responding as selflessly as possible. Which, all things considered, must mean Dunfosters.

And so she said as much.

They thanked her for her deliberation, and behaved in such a manner as to suggest that Emma's word had settled the matter. This was a compliment to her, which she did her best to enjoy; it might be the only reward her integrity would afford her.

But no; for here came her sister, Frances, into the room —and since she was the elder of their daughters, Sir Godfrey and Lady Marlow did her the courtesy of asking her opinion as well.

Frances did not hesitate in her reply. "If it's all the same to you, dear Papa, dearest Mama, I should very much like to return to Graftings. It has been entirely too long since we have settled there."

"By that logic," said Lady Marlow, "we ought to make for Penwether, from which we have been even longer absent."

Frances waved the point aside. "Penwether has waited this long; it can wait longer yet. But I must tell you, Papa, what I miss most keenly about Graftings is Uncle Baldwin's kennels. You know it has been my desire since childhood to take them over. You promised me that I should, someday. Why may not that someday be today?"

Sir Godfrey, reminded of his pledge, was forced to submit to it; though he had made it only because its object had seemed, at the time, no more than a young child's fleeting fancy. He would scarcely have agreed otherwise to allow his fair young daughter sovereignty over the kennels which his late brother, ever prodigal, had had affixed to the property some quarter-century before. A baronet's daughter belonged in a drawing room, not a dog run.

Yet the ensuing years had done nothing to dim Frances's love for all things canine. She scorned society, disdained distaff pursuits, neglected young men, and turned her back on all accomplishments. Her world revolved around her two King Charles spaniels, Dash and Cannon, and she longed for the day when she might make them the progenitors of a great spaniel dynasty.

Thus, as she was the only member of the family whose preference was cast in iron, she carried the day.

The Marlows would return to Graftings.

CHAPTER TWO

Lady Marlow wrote to her sister-in-law, Mrs. Curtis, who lived in Marlhurst, to tell her of their imminent arrival. Mrs. Curtis was delighted to have such interesting news to dispense, and strategized how best to parcel it out to the village.

"It would be simplest first to tell Mrs. Grayson," she explained to her husband—who was not listening—"as she is our nearest neighbor and my dear friend. But she is also an active, interested woman, who would then undertake to relay the news herself, so that inevitably I should come to some household or other, and find that she had been there before me. Thus, though it may put her nose out of joint, I think I must bypass Mrs. Grayson in favor of Mrs. Stanley, who never ventures forth from her house due to her unfortunate terror of highwaymen. I know what you will say, my dear," she added, though her husband quite visibly meant to say nothing; "it is unreasonable to fear highwaymen in a place where there is no highway. But she will not be persuaded, and that is that, so I beg you speak no more of it." Mr. Curtis appeared readily compliant with this request. "Then after Mrs. Stanley, I may just run over two lanes and tell Mrs. Heath, and then I will not be so very far from the parsonage, and I may tell Miss Nesmith, who has no mother and so depends on the kindness of the ladies in town to keep her up-to-date."

Mr. Curtis, whose wife's narrative had formed a kind of low, droning hum in his ears, like that of a hive of unusually industrious bees, had his consciousness snagged by that single word, "parsonage." He looked up from his newspaper and said, "What, my dear? Did you say we have been invited to dine at the parsonage?"

"No, indeed," said Mrs. Curtis with a frown. "You must endeavor to pay greater attention, husband. I said I was to go to the parsonage myself, to tell Miss Nesmith of my brother and sister returning to live at Graftings."

By the time she had finished this clarification, her husband's attention had already drifted back to his broadsheet. He cared only to know whether he might look forward to an evening with the parson, who was one of the very few persons in the village with whom he could agreeably pass an evening; as this was not to be, there was nothing further in his wife's narration to interest him.

"And if I am at the parsonage," continued Mrs. Curtis, applying the full potency of her strategic gift, and furrowing her brow to illustrate as much, "I may have time to dash out to Willmot Lodge and spread the news there. I need only be careful not to be drawn inside for a dish of tea, for such is the way of Willmot Lodge that a dish of tea can easily turn into a commitment of several hours, involving drowning dogs, or collapsed walls, or children's arms pulled out of socket." She sighed in sympathy for a household whose juvenile members so vastly outnumbered those of a rational age.

Then she brightened and resumed her recital. "If I am sufficiently concise, I may arrive back with ample time yet to call on Mrs. Lerner, and then—well, there will only be Mrs. Grayson left, and I daresay no one else will have given her the word. For everyone knows she is my particular friend, and will quite naturally assume I have told her already. Do you see the beauty of my plan, husband? Do you not admire my cunning in conceiving of it?"

Mr. Curtis turned a page of his journal and said, "Your tone just now was interrogative, my dear, though I did not apprehend what you asked. Despite which, you may presume that my reply is whichever answer would please you best."

Mrs. Curtis had been in this position sufficiently often to have learned to set aside her pride, which she knew would never gain satisfaction from any protest she made, no matter how long she made it (as early in her marriage, she had been known to protest very long indeed), and instead to take her husband at his word. "I knew you would commend my particular genius," she said, and she blew him a kiss, took up her shawl, and raced out of the house, nearly knocking a parlour maid off her heels as she swept past.

Mrs. Curtis was more than twenty years younger than her husband, and had had to learn to dampen her own youthful spirits in order to match his sober, careful ways. But she was not so fully converted to the unhurried, deliberate pace of her wedded life, that she did not joy to shirk it whenever she could—as now, with a kernel of gleaming gossip jangling in her purse, and her small, tripping feet carrying her as fleetly around the village as she could wish, so that half her errand was soon accomplished, and in better time than she had hoped.

She found herself at the parsonage, and a little out of breath; but the parson's daughter very kindly invited her in for refreshment—as well she might. Alice Nesmith had few enough friends in the village, which was a thing very curious to Mrs. Curtis, for she was a pretty, witty, amiable creature, who loved news and never tired of hearing more of it. And Mrs. Curtis, who had no friends near to her own age—the other wives in the village being many years her senior—was happy to think her a kindred spirit.

"I do not suppose you will recall," Mrs. Curtis began, after Miss Nesmith had poured her a cup of tea, "because you are *very* young, but until five years ago, my brother, Sir Godfrey Marlow, and his family, lived here in Marlhurst."

"I remember them very well," said Alice, over her own pleasantly steaming cup.

"They have since resided in Wiltshire," Mrs. Curtis continued, "and for the past several months in a market-town, where they had lodgings. (I cannot think what put them in mind to do that.) When they lived here, it was at Graftings, which is the house hid behind all the yew trees; I really think you must remember them."

"Indeed I do," Alice assured her, "as if it were yesterday."

"The house has stood empty since they were last in residence, but what do you think: they are coming back! Indeed they are! I have had a letter...here it is...no, wait, I cannot find it. I had it tucked exactly here, in my reticule...where has it got to? Have I dropped it? Will you call your housekeeper, my dear?...Oh, here she is. Green, would you do me the courtesy of seeing whether a stray letter is to be found lying on the parsonage path? I thank you.—Anyway, my dear Alice, they are to come back, and very soon; I should imagine no later than Wednesday week. And I am sure when you see them, you will remember them all at once."

"I remember them all now, Mrs. Curtis."

"My brother is a baronet, and very stately, and his wife was once a renowned beauty, who still boasts a great dignity. They have three children. Their eldest is Frances, who

Edgar and Emma

I am sorry to say is rather a tom-boy. She does not play or sing or dance, or even sketch or do needlework; she is always out of doors, so that her skin has got quite brown, and we all despair of her ever marrying. She is devoted to her dogs, which she refuses to part from, though I cannot imagine how it must have been, to live in a rented house in a market-town with two such beasts underfoot. I would not have allowed it; but my brother and his wife are very mild. You will see as much when you meet them."

"But I *have* met them. Indeed I remember their mildness."

"Their next child is Emma, who is my favourite, though you must not say I have said so. She is very pretty and accomplished, but has a satirical turn of mind—indeed she struggles to curb her tongue. I know not where she gets it, because, as I have said, her parents are both very mild. My brother, I know, would not curse the storm that knocked his house down around him. But Emma—well, she would have a thing to say about a far slighter inconvenience. She is exactly your age…it would be perplexing were you not to remember her."

"But I do remember her, Mrs. Curtis. Of course I do."

"And finally there is their ward, young Tom, whom they have raised as a son. He is a very curious youth; there is something about him…I suppose the most agreeable way to say it, would be to call him venerable. He reads Law at Cambridge, which I suppose must explain it; his is a cultivated solemnity."

"I agree; I have met him. I see in him exactly what you describe."

"Anyway, I—oh, Green; you say there is no letter? Very well, thank you for having looked.—I expect I must have left it at Mrs. Heath's, which is very tiresome, as it means I

17

will have to stop there on my way home. My dear Alice," she said rising from her chair, "I must go at once. I am yet to stop at Willmot Lodge, and now I have Mrs. Heath to see again as well. I wish I had not left my letter with her. She is such an inexhaustible talker! She will trap me again with one of her interminable stories. I wonder at such persons; they must be utterly lacking in self-governance."

"I will accept your authority on it," said Alice.

"Please advise your dear father of my news," Mrs. Curtis added as she donned her gloves. "He will remember the Marlows. I daresay we will all meet very soon, and I can introduce you to them."

"We know each other already," said Alice as she showed Mrs. Curtis to the door. "But I shall be happy to renew the acquaintance."

As she bustled down the road to Willmot Lodge, Mrs. Curtis suddenly remembered one of her fancies from five years past: that clever, pretty, solitary young Alice Nesmith would make an ideal wife for steadfast, earnest Tom Peake. In fact, she had made rather a project of it, although they had been very young at the time. She would have to take it up again, now that they were of an age at which her influence might yield results.

Even so, it was a singular thing that after all her efforts, Alice should not remember him. Well, that was the carelessness of youth, no doubt. Having wed so young herself, Mrs. Curtis had escaped such consequences. (Though she was not so certain she was entirely thankful for that.)

Introspection made her head ache, so she set aside such thoughts and focused instead on quickening her pace.

She had come very near to Willmot Lodge when she was approached by a gentleman on horseback; who was discovered, as he came nearer, to be Ralph Willmot, the family's second son.

"Good day to you, ma'am," he said when he drew closer, and he tipped his hat. "I take it that you are come to see my mother and father?"

"I am indeed, sir," she said. "But as I have no invitation, I can but hope they are able to receive me."

"My mother is at home," he said, while curbing his horse's restlessness. "I have just left her. She will be glad to see you, I am certain."

"As am I," she said gleefully, "for I come bearing news."

He arched an eyebrow. It was a very attractive gesture; in fact Ralph Willmot was a very attractive man, with cornsilk-yellow hair and riveting blue eyes, and a roguish grin whose effect he clearly knew too well, and deployed without pity. "May I be privileged to hear it?" he asked.

She shook her head. "It is only right that I tell your mother first. But if you are headed into the village, you will hear it spoken of there."

"I am headed to London for several days," he said, smiling and patting his mount's neck to calm her. "As you see, Virago is eager for the exercise; I have rested her well in anticipation of the journey. But consider: as a result of my sojourn in town, it will be nearly a week before I hear your news—by which time indeed it may no longer *be* news. Have pity on a poor traveler." He flashed her his incandescent grin. "I feel certain I am not the first gentleman to beg a favor of you. You must be as generous to me as to all the rest."

Mrs. Curtis could not repress a startled laugh. "You are too shocking, Mr. Willmot; I will not have you speak to me so! My husband would object in the strongest possible terms, were he to hear of it."

"Which he will not, because you will not tell him," he said, with such merry confidence that it quite disarmed reproof. "Though you *will* tell *me* the news you have brought for my mother. You are too kind to do otherwise."

By now, the currents of their conversation had gotten rather more turbulent than Mrs. Curtis was accustomed to; but Ralph Willmot had that effect. There was something about him that was very nearly disorienting. Because she had married at sixteen, she had never learned—had never *had* to learn—how to deflect, or even to resist, the flirtations of a handsome man.

Nor did she feel she needed to learn it now; her wedding ring was her protection. Doubtless Ralph Willmot considered it so as well, and felt safe in speaking so provocatively to her; which meant that his blandishments were the merest flattery. And if they pleased her, and did no one else any harm, how could anyone object—even her husband? Could a man who never vouchsafed her a word of commendation, deny her the pleasure of hearing pretty, empty words from a trifling acquaintance?

And yet…all this conjecture had the effect of throwing her much-vaunted news into a more humbling perspective. Compared to the way Ralph Willmot made her feel—like she was thrillingly skirting the outer perimeter of scandal— the intelligence of a family moving back into the neighborhood was tepid stuff indeed.

"Of course I will take pity on you, sir," she said with a gentle smile. "It really is not so much to fuss about; merely that my sister and brother—the Marlows; you may remember them—are soon to come back to Graftings."

A look passed over Ralph Willmot's face; but it was a look she was unable to read. It did seem, on evidence, to be one of pleasure; but from what the pleasure derived, it was not possible to tell.

"These are happy tidings," he said. "We want variety in the neighborhood, and they will be just the thing."

"I feel the same."

"I look forward to meeting them again. And I thank you, ma'am, for the gift of your confidence. I shall keep it unto death; or at least, until you give me leave to speak of it."

Again she shrieked a laugh; and was immediately embarrassed for it. She felt herself a silly schoolgirl.

He tipped his hat once more, and rode off.

She watched him go; then she turned and continued her trek to Willmot Lodge. But she could no longer enjoy the exercise; the very air about her was agitated by her encounter with Ralph. He was, she realized, entirely too free in his manner, too assured of the potency of his charm. Far better that he were married, with a wife to steady him and tame his exuberance.

As she plodded on, Mrs. Curtis remembered that in earlier days she had had an idea of matching him to her niece, Emma. They would make such a pretty pair, both so handsome and so flaxen, like they were both carved from a single block of spruce. And now she recalled as well that towards the end of her last stay in Marlhurst, Emma had grown very interested in the Willmots, eager to know more of them and to see them whenever the opportunity arose.

Well then; Mrs. Curtis would put her mind to it, now that the girl was coming back to Graftings. It would give her two projects to which she might devote her copious energies: pairing Alice Nesmith to Tom Peake, and Emma Marlow to Ralph Willmot.

❧

"This is good news indeed," said Mrs. Willmot as they sat in her parlour. "The Marlows were always a welcome addition to our society. I am very glad to know they will soon resume a part in it." It was just the two of them, and of course Patience, the Willmots' eldest child—a plain young woman of twenty-eight who had abandoned all hope of finding a husband, donned her cap, and devoted herself to being her mother's companion; in which capacity she now sat, off to one side, quietly working her needle.

Mrs. Curtis, who was three years her junior, often wondered at Patience's folly in giving up so soon; in her place, she would yet have been canvassing every eligible male in the eighty-three English counties, and a plain face would not have stopped her from securing one of them, though the Devil himself might bar the way. There were times when she thought Patience must have taken her Christian name too much to heart. Far better had the Willmots baptized her Charity. Or Hope. Or Delilah.

"I knew you would be pleased," said Mrs. Curtis to Mrs. Willmot, "and you must promise to pass the news to your good husband, and to attach my fond regards." She clutched her reticule as if preparing to rise to her feet. Time had a habit of moving more slowly at Willmot Lodge, so that one might feel one had passed a pleasant half-hour therein, only to emerge and find the sun dipping below the horizon and owls hooting in the trees; and therefore one must be decisive in making an escape from it.

But Mrs. Willmot forestalled her by gesturing to a vase to her left and saying, "Patience, these wildflowers have lost their bloom; will you take them to Davis and ask her to replace them?"

Edgar and Emma

"You always take such care with your flowers," Mrs. Curtis said, to keep the chatter going as Patience crossed the room. "I wish I had your touch. Each time I enter the Lodge, I feel like I have come upon Covent Garden market. Of course I have never seen that place; I longed to do so, when I was a girl, and begged my governess to take me; but she said it was no place for a lady, and I daresay she was right. But I have never yet lost the yearning; I suppose that is very silly, at my age."

Patience, vase in hand, quietly exited the room, and Mrs. Curtis, having run out of chatter, began to rise as well, to make her own escape. But Mrs. Willmot seemed oblivious to her readiness to depart, and fixed her in place by posing more questions about the returning neighbors.

"And do you know," she asked, "whether Miss Emma Marlow will accompany the family?"

"Of course she will," Mrs. Curtis said, reluctantly re-settling herself. "Why should she do otherwise?"

"It occurred to me that she might, in these past five years, have found herself a husband, and acquired an establishment of her own."

"Oh! no. I assure you, Emma is yet unmarried. I would certainly have told you so, if it were otherwise."

Mrs. Willmot—a very large woman, with rosy cheeks and an ample breast—visibly relaxed, which involved so much unbending of her anxiously constricted spine and shoulders, that the air in the room seemed to grow more compressed. "How happy I am to hear it!" she said. "For I have always thought there was some particular interest between her and my Edgar."

Mrs. Curtis barked a laugh. "I think you are mistaken, ma'am! It is Emma and Ralph, rather, between whom there is an observable keenness."

23

"Is it so?" asked Mrs. Willmot with a look of genuine surprise. "Ah! well, you are much nearer their age than I, Mrs. Curtis, so I must credit your judgment. And I confess I care not overmuch; with so many sons to find wives for, it is all the same to me whether Miss Emma Marlow settles on one or another."

"She shall settle on one, certainly," said Mrs. Curtis. "It would not surprise me, indeed, to learn that it was she who instigated this return to Graftings, for the specific purpose of renewing her childhood fancy."

"I shall encourage it, then," said Mrs. Willmot with a nod. "Anything to prompt the children to move on. Even with Richard away at Eton, and Amy with my sister Clayton, there are too many on hand to provide me a moment's repose."

As if to illustrate the veracity of this statement, the youngest Willmot daughters—a pair of twins, Mary-Anne and Lucy-Anne, both thirteen—burst into the room in full cry, and appealed to their mother to settle a dispute over a box of pencils, the possession of which was apparently so vital that each girl professed herself certain to die from the lack of it.

It was during the initial arguments in this suit that Mrs. Curtis quietly slipped away.

CHAPTER THREE

It was one of the features of the time, by which everyone professed to be shocked but which everyone accepted none the less, that the position of clergyman had been so thoroughly degraded that it had become a profession instead of a calling. In practice it was little more than a repository for second or third sons of the gentry, or for those gentlemen whose ambitions did not incline to government or the law, but who required an occupation all the same. Everyone knew, or knew of, an ostensible man of the cloth who was transparently a man of the world, and many poor souls in parishes across the realm went from cradle to grave with the benefit of no divine guidance but that obtained from a minister whose spirituality was as easily put on, and taken off again, as his cassock.

The Rev. Mr. Nesmith, who held the Marlhurst living, was not one such. He abided by the principles set down by the Church, and was resolute in his insistence that all who formed his congregation do likewise. He exhibited, however, little of the joy one might expect to find in a man who kept faith with the Gospels, and in fact seemed often quite openly vexed; and it was believed that the failings of his flock, rather than moving him to pity, prompted him to wroth. He was unwavering in his religious convictions, but lacked a corresponding sympathy for imperfect, imprecise, impenetrable human nature that might have made him of genuine service to his parishioners.

Despite this, they were proud of their firebrand of a parson, and admired the sternness of his aspect and the swiftness of his judgment; but they could not help, at those moments when his fury blazed a little too uncomfortably near, and singed their self-regard, wishing instead for a bland, fat curate who would solemnize their weddings and baptize their babies, and spend the rest of his time in his garden, doting on his hollyhocks. For there was never a moment in which Mr. Nesmith appeared to ease his rectitude, or defer the pursuit of his duties to accommodate the pleasures of company. (It was this which made him so valued a dinner partner to Mr. Curtis: the parson showed up, spoke little, ate briskly, and then departed—for Mr. Curtis, a model houseguest in every respect.) If asked to justify his rigorous probity—and no one had yet dared—he would have replied that there was a war between good and evil that had been raging for two thousand years, in which they all served as foot soldiers, and thus must be ever vigilant against the next iniquitous sally. The romance of this vision could be stirring; but the reality of living with it day to day tended to wear.

There was but one person in all his flock on whom his energy and bombast fell flat, and that was his daughter. He had been lucky in his wife—the late Mrs. Nesmith had been a meek, compliant soul, who took direction from him in all things, and submitted to his will with never a word of protest or reproach—but he was unlucky in his child, because Alice took entirely after him, and not at all after her mother. The girl was proud, willful, fearless, and utterly dogged.

Edgar and Emma

This would not have been a problem were she not unlike him in one troubling respect: she was worldly. Or rather she aspired to worldliness; for she had seen little enough of the world yet to manage it. From her earliest days she was the despair of her father, with her attraction to all that was bright and glittering and gay. She begrudged every day she was forced to spend in the country, in the household of a dour, sober man, toiling like a dray horse on his behalf, while her beauty and charm were at their zenith.

But she was clever, and had devised a plan of escape. The Willmots were the richest of the families accessible to her, and they had a plenitude of sons; she intended to wed one of them. At first she had singled out Ralph, as he was the nearest to her in temperament. Her initial attentions to him were amply recompensed, and after a few weeks there was a general expectation of an attachment between them. But as their acquaintance deepened, she became increasingly aware of a streak of wildness in him. He was prodigal and profligate, burning through money as though it were tinder and allowing his eye to rove wherever it would. Alice was canny enough to understand that if she could not control him now, when youth and novelty were to her advantage, she would be much less likely to do so after they had been wed a span of years. Disaster lay at the end of their road together. Accordingly she behaved more coolly towards him. Without her encouragement, their flirtation ran its natural course, and so skillfully had she orchestrated it that they remained the best of friends.

She then turned her mind to Edgar. He was neither so handsome nor so dashing as Ralph, but he *was* the heir to the Willmot fortune; and given his natural humility, she was certain she could exercise sufficient authority over him. Let him but show the slightest inclination, and before he knew it, she would have him draping her in jewels, housing her on a fashionable street in town, and traveling to and fro in their very own barouche.

But alas, Edgar did *not* show the slightest inclination. Try as she might to dazzle him with her bountiful charms, he remained remote, indeed nearly oblivious. It was some time before she perceived that the means to fix his attention were not the same as had fixed his brother's; an entirely new strategy was called for.

She subsequently learned, through interrogation of his sisters (expertly disguised as idle chatter), that Edgar's passion was for history, and specifically the Classical period. And so she feigned a shared enthusiasm, as a result of which she had had to endure a number of very long evenings, cornered by him at some gathering or other, listening to him rhapsodize Pericles the Great or Scipio Africanus, when she would rather have engaged herself in livelier pursuits like gossiping, or dancing, or playing spillikins. Indeed, she would rather have sat quietly and done nothing at all. The boredom of her own blank thoughts was preferable to the clanging dullness of the Seven Against Thebes.

So very tiresome did she find these occasions, and so slowly did Edgar respond to them (his manner towards her had but warmed by the barest perceptible degree) that she had begun to consider abandoning him for the next Willmot brother down—Richard; but he was away at Eton—or the one after that—David; but he was not yet sixteen.

Now Mrs. Curtis had come and delivered the news that caused her to take up the reins she had dropped, and once more commit herself to the conquest of Edgar Willmot's heart. The return of the Marlows to Graftings was not an event to be regarded blithely, because there were two daughters to that house, both unmarried, and of an age with herself. Even more alarmingly, during the entirety of their acquaintance, Alice had known Edgar to speak the name of only one other young lady in her presence—and that was Miss Emma Marlow.

Alice was a keen observer of her fellow man, and she had a long memory besides. She well recalled an event from five years prior, when this very Miss Emma Marlow, having injured herself on a walk far from home, had been carried back to Graftings by Edgar himself, who had heard her cry out and gone to rescue her. The story had been briefly sensational in Marlhurst, and for almost a fortnight had been told and re-told at many gatherings, with many inevitable embellishments. (In the original account, the girl had been affrighted by a small snake; by the time the story reached its pinnacle, the offending creature had swelled into a ravenous wolf, which Edgar had warded off with a flaming fagot.)

There was little doubt in Alice's mind that Edgar had enjoyed his fleeting reputation as a romantic hero. He would never say so; but as the older, less dashing, more solemn brother of Ralph Willmot, he can only have relished having the sunny light of approbation cast on him for a change, in place of the usual glazed-over gaze of disregard. In his mind, Miss Emma Marlow must forever be associated with this phenomenon; and his pleasure in its memory would only be augmented by her presence—especially if she had grown up pretty. Which seemed likely; Alice remembered her as having been quite fetching at thirteen.

Her scheme for Edgar was not yet in certain peril; for while Mrs. Curtis had not mentioned a husband for either Marlow girl—and as their aunt, she would be sure to know of any—it remained possible that Miss Emma Marlow had acquired a suitor sometime during her absence, and perhaps even come to an understanding with him. It was unlike Mrs. Curtis to neglect to mention such a thing, but it was not an impossibility. Alice must hope soon to learn of an attachment between Miss Emma Marlow and Mr. Some-body-or-other, the disappointment of which might make Edgar Willmot more amenable to her pity, and to her comfort.

Time alone would tell. In the interim, she must gird her loins and prepare to do battle. But even more pressingly, she must see to her father's dinner. Both the cook and the housekeeper at the parsonage were very old, and neither sufficiently respected her authority. Perhaps her youth was to blame—although there were mistresses of greater house-holds who were younger than she. More likely it was that both servants could see that Alice's interest in the house was chiefly as a place to flee, and scaled down their indus-triousness accordingly. Why strive to excel in one's duties for a mistress whose gaze was always turned longingly out the window?

And yet if her father were unhappy with his dinner, it was Alice who would suffer a rebuke, not the staff. So she made certain that all was in order, and was rewarded, in mid-meal, with his thanks...though in truth the repast comprised no more than a cold consommé, French bread and cheese, and a joint of beef. Mr. Nesmith embraced plain eating, declaring it consonant with his office. His one indulgence was a glass of dry sack before the meal—which, as it softened his mood as well as stimulated his appetite, Alice wholly approved.

Their dinnertime conversations were never very scintil-lating; in fact Mr. Nesmith would sometimes carry a book to the table so that he might continue his researches unin-terrupted. When he did not, he might catechize Alice on her own studies, in which she was invariably delinquent; but she had learned over the years how to frame a non-answer that appeased him. It took no special cleverness on her part, for he was often willing to be deceived, it being the far better choice than cornering her into confessing a half-truth, and thus prompting her into open rebellion.

Tonight, however, he felt more voluble than usual. "I believe you have had some company today, my dear," he said as he carved himself a slice of meat. "I heard quite a chorus of voices from my study."

"I am sorry if we disturbed you, Father," she said.

"I was not in the least disturbed. Such was the steadiness of the din that after a quarter-hour I ceased to hear it at all. But your visitors were certainly a garrulous lot."

"In point of fact, Father, I had but one caller today; Mrs. Curtis."

He put down his knife and fork in amazement. "Indeed? But I distinctly heard competing voices. What a prodigious talker that women is; she can even overlap herself. Yet it was kind of her to visit you. Did she come on any special purpose?"

"She brought news, Father. It seems the Marlows are soon to return to Graftings."

He nodded in approval as he chewed; and when he had swallowed, he said, "I will welcome them. For a baronet, Sir Godfrey displays a very commendable humility. He will be an example to the strutting young men hereabouts. Does his family accompany him?"

"Yes, sir; that is, his wife and two daughters. I believe his ward will be here but briefly; he then returns to Cambridge."

Mr. Nesmith looked contemplative. "Neither girl is married, then?"

"No, sir. Though Mrs. Curtis gives me to understand that both are out."

This pointed reference was rather provocative of Alice, for she longed to be out herself; but in the absence of her mother, this would require a female relative coming to stay, to perform the necessary chaperoning. Mr. Nesmith, alas, was unlikely ever to assent to this, for he thought the practice of introducing young ladies to society—often making an elaborate business of formally presenting them to persons they had known their whole lives—a very silly one. Father and daughter had contended over the matter many times; but of late Alice had largely given it up. Because even were her father to agree to it, her only female relative was her mother's sister, Mrs. Scope—a woman whose religious fervor burned even more fiercely than her brother-in-law's. Indeed she made him seem by comparison a debauched idolator. Mr. Nesmith, who disapproved of excess in all things, including fidelity to heaven, had once, when his guard was down, dropped a shocking hint that he suspected Mrs. Scope of having gone over to Methodism.

On this occasion, Alice's confrontational remark on the matter sailed as cleanly over her father's head as if she had pitched her words at the rafters, not at him. Something else had occurred to him that consumed his thoughts.

"Graftings," he said. "I believe that is where the disgraced housemaid is employed."

"Violet Cutler?" Alice said.

He frowned. "Is it necessary to clarify, my dear? Will you now tell me that our humble village is host to more than one?"

"No indeed," she said, and she felt her face go red. "Forgive me, Father."

"I prefer that her name remain unspoken at my dinner table. That is all."

She sensed an opportunity to vex him by pointing out an inconstancy in his convictions. "But have you not said, Father, that as a daughter of Christ she is to be forgiven her transgression, and not ejected from the community?"

But he was not to be goaded. "Indeed I have, child; for what is Christ's dictate to us, but that we forgive others as we ourselves would be forgiven?" He beamed condescension at her. "Yet for her part, the girl must show gratitude for her forgiveness, by forever going about with her head lowered in shame, and speaking only when spoken to, and even then never presuming to meet the eyes of those whom she addresses. It is simply a matter of showing contrition, and of not offending those who have managed, in the face of manifold temptations, to conduct themselves with greater propriety."

"Of course, Father," said Alice. But she could not remember such stipulations being set forth in the Gospels, and she had been made to read them many times through. It was very like her father, that he should endorse Violet Cutler's absolution while concurrently seeing to it that she never be allowed to forget the crime of which she had been absolved. Alice sometimes wondered whether he privately thought that Christ had been entirely too whimsical in his pronouncements, and would have liked the opportunity to amend one, or two, or all of them.

"And that is very much to my point," he said now. "Such a person may not be the most suitable housemaid in an establishment boasting two maiden daughters. It lacks decorum." He took up another mouthful of beef, and when he had consumed it he added, "I don't like to presume to lecture a baronet on private matters. Doubtless he and his lady will settle it simply enough between them, when it is brought to their attention. If not, I'll very gently have a word."

And with that, Mr. Nesmith felt that he had exposed his innocent young daughter to quite enough deliberation on so sordid a subject. The fate of Violet Cutler was a valuable object lesson for all the town's young ladies, but there was a point beyond which consideration of it bordered on prurience. Accordingly he changed the subject to an epidemic of loose bowels currently afflicting the parsonage sheep, which kept father and daughter pleasantly occupied until the end of the meal, when each retired to solitary pursuits.

CHAPTER FOUR

Sir Godfrey's confidence that any of his houses was ready to receive him, turned out to be misplaced; for when the family arrived at Graftings they found much in want. The garden and parkland were in excellent state, due to the ministrations of their exemplary groundskeeper, Carr; but the house itself was in some disarray. Three rooms were still beneath cloth, including the breakfast room, which was very inconvenient, and those that had been made ready were not scrupulously clean. Emma noted with dismay that her mother's traveling coat, which was very long, left a visible trail on the dusty floor of one of the upstairs rooms.

Hicks, the housekeeper, followed Lady Marlow on her inspection, but with what Emma thought was inadequate humility for the magnitude of her failings. Indeed, Hicks seemed instead to expect to draw Lady Marlow into sympathy with her, for the many frustrations and indignities she had suffered on the family's behalf.

"It is the fault of the young people today, my lady," she said. "They none of them have the discipline, nor indeed the desire, to work. I have been through four laundry maids in total since last you resided here, which you will note is almost one for every year. And heaven knows I have lost count of the hall boys. One of them did not wait for the dignity of being dismissed, but departed of his own volition, and I am still not certain he did not take something away with him to make the adventure worth his while, though I have been over the silver and plate several times since and can find nothing lacking. And I beg you will not ask me to begin listing the defects of the housemaid, but I will note that she has got herself into a rather…unfortunate circumstance"—here she shot a quick glance at Emma and Frances, as if to gauge whether they took her meaning, which Emma certainly did—"and is unable to work to her fullest capacity…not that her fullest capacity is much to speak of. Perhaps I ought to have discharged her, but she is very popular in the village—I daresay too much so, given the evidence—and it would reflect badly on the family were we to cut loose a young girl in such obvious distress, and leave her with no other means of support."

"Has she no parents?" asked Lady Marlow, leading the way into the sewing room.

"There is a mother—such as she is," said Hicks, following with brisk steps and coming up behind Lady Marlow in time to see her run her gloved hand along the upper edge of a moulding. The result was not felicitous. Lady Marlow frowned, and Hicks hastened to continue her reply. "She has a reputation for light fingers; indeed Mr. Nichols the fruit seller will not allow her within six yards of his shop, and has been known to clear her from his premises with the aid of a well-aimed quince."

Lady Marlow sighed and turned back to the doorway. "I think this maid had better remain below stairs. It won't do for my daughters to be exposed to a girl in her condition."

"My very thought, my lady," said Hicks eagerly. "Indeed I was on the very point of suggesting exactly that."

Lady Marlow cut short her inspection of the house and returned to the drawing room to report to her husband; who immediately set his valet, Samson, the task of aiding

Hicks in putting the house to order. Samson returned later, just as the family had gathered for tea, to assure them that all was well in hand, and to offer his private opinion that, "Had Mrs. Hicks devoted half the energy to her duties that she has committed to composing her defense for having failed in them, the latter endeavor would not have been necessary."

This was not the homecoming they had anticipated; but despite their exalted rank, Sir Godfrey and Lady Marlow were very even-tempered people (how else had they managed to live in close lodgings in Chipping Norton?) and were soon quite at their ease. Indeed Sir Godfrey felt sufficiently pleased with his return to order the bells rung, and to distribute ninepence among the ringers.

After tea had concluded, Frances could be contained no longer and tore from the house with Dash and Cannon loping after her, to assess the repair of the long-neglected kennels. Sir Godfrey retired to his library, there to reacquaint himself with his collection and pass an hour or two in quiet study. Lady Marlow went up to her room, claiming that the journey had tired her.

Tom had not yet arrived; there had been no room for him in the carriage, so it was decided he would follow on horseback, which allowed him to delay his own departure until it best suited him. He was not expected until dinner.

This left Emma on her own, with nothing very much to do. Her room was still being unpacked, so she could not retire to it; nor could she occupy herself with a book, for hers were in her trunks, and her father, when in his library, was to be disturbed for nothing less pressing than a French invasion—and perhaps not even that, depending on whether it were cavalry or merely infantry.

It was by now a few hours since they had arrived at the house, so that Emma had recovered from the exhaustion of the journey, and not only could face the outdoors again, but found herself eager to do so. She settled on taking a walk. The exercise would clear her head of the dullness that had been lodged there by the endless jostling of the road, and then made worse by the perpetual braying of Hicks's self-exoneration. It was growing rather late in the day, but she needn't wander too long; she might go only as far as the kennels, to see how Frances fared.

She left the room to fetch her shawl, and was surprised to find herself not alone in the corridor. A girl stood at the end of it, silhouetted against the window; and even in profile it was clear that she was crying.

"I beg your pardon," Emma said. "Are you not well?"

The girl started, and stepped away from the window; and Emma could see that she was very young—as young as herself—and that the front of her skirt protruded due to a visible swelling beneath.

"The delinquent housemaid," Emma told herself.

"Thank you, miss," the girl said; "I am very well, miss; my apologies, miss."

But it was plainly evident that she was not very well at all. In point of fact, her agitation quite shocked Emma, who was jarred into an unpleasant realization of just how sheltered her own life had been. She had come to think herself rather experienced, for all the varieties of human behavior she had witnessed on the streets of Chipping Norton; but she had never in her life encountered anything like this private anguish, which was pitched to so high a degree, and was so nakedly unabashed. Emma could not begin to imagine the degradation necessary to reduce someone to such utter unselfconsciousness.

She thought to offer a consoling word, but before she could compose one Hicks appeared from around the corner, her face a paper-white mask of fury.

"Violet!" she exclaimed. "Was it not an hour agone that I bade you venture no more upstairs?"

"But I have not cleared the tea service," the girl said, her voice unsteady and very pitiful to hear.

"I have come myself on that very purpose," said Hicks. "Now, off with you! Back below stairs where you belong!"

Violet scuttled past Emma, whimpering as she went; and when she was out of sight the housekeeper smiled grimly at her young mistress.

"My apologies, miss," she said. "You should not have had to suffer that encounter; it was your mother's sole admonition to me. I hope you will not think it necessary to tell her of it."

Emma ignored this plea for secrecy. "She seems very much discomposed," she said, looking in the direction the girl had gone.

"As well she might, in her difficulty," said Hicks indignantly. "I'm sure she ought to have considered the consequences before she gave herself over to folly."

"Her name is Violet, you say?" asked Emma.

"Yes—but there is no need for you to learn it, miss. She will trouble you no further. I daresay she will henceforth be invisible to you. You need never know she is beneath the same roof."

Emma did not find this as comforting as Hicks seemed to think she ought.

"Is there anything else, miss?" the housekeeper asked, as though it had been Emma who had summoned her, and not she who had interposed herself.

"No, thank you, Hicks," she said. But when she turned to go, Emma said, "Wait—yes. I wonder—if you have a moment—whether you might satisfy my curiosity on a small matter."

Hicks turned back and looked at her with wary interest. "Curiosity, miss?"

"Yes." It had occurred to her, during the long carriage ride, when she had been so interminably trapped with her own thoughts, that at twenty-five Edgar Willmot might well have taken a wife. She was determined to have it not be so, but could not shake a sense of dread all the same. "I wonder whether there have been many marriages made, in the time we have been gone," she asked.

"Oh, bless me, yes, quite some number," said Hicks, and she proceeded not only to cite them, but to provide the prevailing opinion of each match, as to whether *he* was worthy of *her* or vice-versa, or who had married solely for fortune, and who had taken to drink in regret, and so on— an oration that lasted until Frances came barging back in from the kennels, her shoes caked with mud and her dogs no less so, flushed of face and yet happy, and declaring that there was not so much rot as she had feared, and that a carpenter would need no more than a few days to bring it all to order.

Mere moments later Tom arrived and entered the house beaming good cheer. Sir Godfrey, hearing his voice, came out to greet him; and with a sigh Emma gave up her project of a walk, re-hung her shawl, and rejoined her family.

But she was not dispirited. Because in the litany of names the housekeeper had related in her long marital chronicle, Edgar Willmot's had not been mentioned.

CHAPTER FIVE

"The Marlows are in residence at Graftings," said Mrs. Willmot. "We will call on them tomorrow afternoon, to congratulate them on their return."

"I can ride over in the morning," her husband volunteered, "and ascertain from Sir Godfrey whether that would be welcome."

"You are very kind, Mr. Willmot, but such exertion is unnecessary. Mrs. Curtis informs me that the family will be at home, Lady Marlow has sent a card confirming it, and Mrs. Grayson has already announced her plan to call at three o'clock; so I thought we might time our own arrival for half-past the hour."

"I can see," said Mr. Willmot, "that the ladies of Marlhurst are, as usual, several paces ahead of the gentlemen. Very well. I am at your service, my dear. Command me or no, as you will."

"I will indeed command you, since you are so agreeable. For I am uncertain as to how many of the children ought to accompany us. I pray you will advise me."

Mr. Willmot sat back in his chair and gave his wife a very satisfactory show of considering the matter with due gravity. It was ten o'clock, an hour at which the younger members of the household had gone to bed, leaving their elders free to take a glass of sherry or port and enjoy, if fleetingly, the absence of riot and tumult. Mr. Willmot had already downed one glass, which had rendered him introspective; his second might render him inert. So he had better answer his wife now; and after a moment's further thought he peered over his spectacles at her and said, "Why may not they all come with us?"

"Graftings is a small house," said Mrs. Willmot, "and the Marlows have but two daughters and a ward. I do not like to overwhelm them."

"Surely we are not so many as to inconvenience a baronet and his lady!"

"They are not so grand as you remember; and you, sir, are accustomed to our company, and forget the sensational effect we can have on those whom we descend upon unawares."

"But the Marlows will not be unawares; nor are they unfamiliar with the bounty of our progeny."

"That is certainly true; but time may have blunted their memory of exactly how many they are. Mrs. Curtis, who is Sir Godfrey's own sister, and an acquaintance I have often welcomed in this very house, often confuses the number. I have known her to say as little as seven and as many as thirteen."

"Mrs. Curtis is not so fortunate as to have a child of her own," observed Mr. Willmot, who did not greatly care for that lady, "or she would not have wished you so many as that." In truth, although he loved his children, the idea of four more of them made him go quite pale.

"It must also be said," his wife continued, "that when last we saw the Marlows, many of our offspring were very young. Now five years have passed, and they have grown large and strapping, with great, booming voices."

Mr. Willmot did not like this characterization of his darlings. "Perhaps Graftings has sufficient hitching posts to which we can tether them," he said sharply. "And for refreshment, we may pitch some hay their way."

Mrs. Willmot frowned at him. "Come now; there is no need to be satirical. I only mean that our children fill much more of a room today, than they did when last the Marlows saw them."

"You are too nice on the Marlows' behalf, I think. Do I not recall that their eldest daughter is a famous lover of dogs? She kept two in the house with her, I believe. Great, rambunctious beasts. Now that she is older, I suspect she has graduated to a full...what is the word, for a multiplicity of canines? Horde? Pride? Cabal?"

"The term is 'pack,' " came a voice from across the room. In her quiet corner, where she sat nursing her thimbleful of madeira, Patience—the sole adult child at home tonight, and thus permitted to share in the evening's refreshment—now chose to interject herself into the discussion, before her father and mother could fall into contentiousness. She had served this function many times before, and knew how to head off incipient disputation.

"If I may remind you, dear Mama, dearest Papa," she continued, "Amy is with Aunt Clayton, and three of the boys are away as well. So we are at present seven, not eleven; a number much less to be feared."

"By heaven, you're right," said her father. "Why is it, Mrs. Willmot, that neither you nor I happened to consider that?"

"We are not so clever as our children," said his wife. "At least, I'm sure I am not. You, sir, I suspect are distracted by thoughts of industry and the affairs of the realm."

"Indeed so," he said; though in fact, before his wife had interrupted him with her proposition to call on the Marlows, his principal thought had been of when he might next slip away to visit an obliging young seamstress who lived with her mother on the village outskirts. Mr. Willmot had gone from taking pride in his wife's extraordinary fecundity, when first they were wed, to now, many years later, living in abject fear of it; so that as a precaution, he enjoyed himself as much as prudence allowed outside the dangerous terrain of her fertile embrace.

With the matter thus settled, each member of the trio fell into private thoughts. Indeed Mr. Willmot fell into private *slumber*, as he was wont to do, and his wife and daughter would risk no further conversation, lest it wake him. When they had finished their own dainty libations, they went upstairs, leaving Mr. Willmot to the care of his valet, Hastings, who never failed, by some means Mrs. Willmot never cared to inquire into, and her husband even less so, to arrange it so that when Mr. Willmot awoke the next morning he would be in his nightshirt and cap, in his own bed, in his own room.

Alone in her bedchamber, Patience sat before her mirror and brushed out her hair before retiring for the night. It was very long hair, black and silken, and she was immoderately proud of it—perhaps it was the only immoderate thing about her. Again, as every night, she lamented that no one would ever see her hair in its unpinned splendour and admire it as much as she did herself; not even her sister Amy, who had shared this room before their Aunt Clayton (who had fixed on Amy as her favourite) persuaded the family to allow her to take her on as a companion. With so many children already bulging at the rafters, the Willmots did not require too strenuous an argument before they submitted. And for a time, Patience was very glad to have a room to herself—a very wonderful luxury, for a girl her age, in her situation.

But it had seemed less wonderful once she had accepted that her situation would never alter. Then the luxury of having a room all her own became instead the curse of that being all she would *ever* call her own. Yet she had not acted precipitously in making it so; for she had twice been disappointed in love, allowing herself to feel earnest affection for men who did not choose to return the favor, and she meant never again to risk such injury to her heart. Thus, pitying her mother (who felt the loss of Amy much more keenly than she had imagined she would), it had seemed right for Patience to close the door on all hope of matrimony, and take her place at her mother's side, as her confidant and comforter.

But she had done this at three-and-twenty, at which point her memory of Tom Peake had been of a boy of fifteen…an intelligent, somewhat grave boy of fifteen, to be sure; but a boy of fifteen all the same. When she next saw him—just the previous summer—the change in him was astonishing. He rode into Marlhurst one morning, bearing a communication from Sir Godfrey to his groundskeeper at Graftings, and stayed long enough to pay his respects to all the Marlows' principal connections in the village.

This quite naturally brought him to Willmot Lodge— accompanied by his Aunt Curtis, who was effusive in her praise of him—and he was reintroduced to the family, who scarcely recognized him. He was taller by several inches, and his jaw had attractively squared; his voice had deepened and his manner softened. He behaved with the utmost courtesy, though without much warmth; there was very much a sense of his withholding his private self from display. And in truth Patience, although impressed by the improvement in him, did not feel much drawn to him; she found him rather distant.

But then something happened that galvanized her in quite a different way. Mrs. Willmot said something mildly stupid, and Mrs. Curtis replied in such a way as to compound the original stupidity many times over; and Tom Peake turned to Patience, and gave her such a look—a look of sympathy and understanding; a look that said, "We must not laugh," while acknowledging that this was something both very much wished to laugh at—that had Patience not been seated, she might have been knocked back on her heels. It was the most intimate moment she had ever shared with a man, the only time one of that sex had looked at her and no one else, and established—however briefly—a small space which they alone inhabited, in perfect concord.

She had not seen Tom since, but had thought of him often; and the prospect of meeting him the very next day was very exciting.

It was all foolishness, of course; she was a woman of eight-and-twenty, who had removed herself from the marriage market. He was a young man of just twenty, the ward of a baronet, with a future ahead of him that comprised many dances, many dalliances, many courtships and kisses, before he settled on a wife. There was no reason that he should look at her; none at all.

And yet…she very much hoped he should look all the same.

CHAPTER SIX

On the morning of the day set aside for callers, Emma found herself in a state of nervous expectation. She took great care with her dress, so that she might be seen to best advantage when the visitors arrived; but had then the difficult task of maintaining that appearance of freshness as the hours wore on. This was not made easier by Frances, who, in high excitement at the prospect seeing so many old friends (especially Mr. Denham, who had promised to bring his Labrador retriever, Magnate), ran about the house in an attempt to groom the spaniels, who very much wished to remain exactly as they were. At one point Cannon, the male of the pair, tore past Emma with such brusqueness that Emma spun for a moment like a top, and was in peril of falling over; and though she steadied herself at the last, her hair had come out of curl, which called for immediate repair. This required the services of her lady's maid, Jenny, who had just sat down to her own, long-deferred breakfast, and was loath to leave it; so that both mistress and maid were in sullen spirits as they gathered before the vanity mirror to re-set the drooping locks.

Emma's next gauntlet was lunch, which was a humble enough affair—a brace of pheasants, a tierce of hares, poached oysters, plovers' eggs in aspic, white soup, gooseberry cheese, tomato soufflé, cherry-water ice, and a nougat almond cake—but Sir Godfrey, perhaps out of a heightened sense of occasion, proposed a glass of wine instead of the usual ale. The introduction of this novelty nearly proved disastrous, for while relating an anecdote from the previous day, Tom gestured in such a manner as to topple Emma's wineglass. She was able to twist out of the way of the spill, though it was some minutes before she was certain none of the droplets had marred her gown (an investigation that again required the summoning of Jenny, who was by now persuaded that she was being tormented on purpose). Yet afterward, when she resumed her seat—or rather, when she took her place in the new, dry chair that was brought for her—she was sufficiently vexed to lose the governance of her tongue. "I am perfectly willing to go out and hurl myself into the trough," she told her family in a very sharp manner, "if that is what will satisfy you all to leave me in peace." She had no sooner made this offer than her father bade her mind her temper.

Her anxiety turned into open agony once the calls recommenced, for at any moment she expected the Willmots to be introduced, and to see he whom she had so long yearned to meet again. He would walk through the door, taller, no doubt, and even more regal in bearing, but with perhaps—was it so very much to wish for?—a momentary softening of his look when his eyes first settled on her. Or instead of a softening, a slight perplexity, only resolved when Lady Marlow said, "And of course you recall my youngest daughter, Emma," at which his eyes would widen in astonishment, and he would say, "Miss Emma Marlow! but I would not have known you. How very altered you are; you left us a girl, and you return to us a woman."

Well…perhaps that *was* a bit much to wish for.

Edgar and Emma

Every time the door to the parlor opened, her heart leapt in her breast; but when the footman entered and announced someone else entirely, she sank again into despondency. How those first few hours tried her—sitting quietly through the visits of the Heaths (he had grown fatter; she, leaner), the Barrets (who had done the opposite), and Mrs. Buckley (who had acquired a new husband and become Mrs. Lynch).

Mr. Denham followed; and on his entry Emma took refuge behind the furniture, to be out of the way for Magnate's introduction to Dash and Cannon. Alas, for all his size, the Labrador was affrighted by the yapping spaniels, and dove for safety behind the very divan Emma had chosen; upon which the two spaniels leapt to confront him from the other side, so that Emma found herself pinned between the awful, snarling beasts and their larger victim, who was happy to use her as a barrier. Were that not amply exasperating in itself, she had also to contend with the laughter of all the others at her predicament.

"They have attempted the ruin of my hair," she thought defiantly; "then my gown; and now my life and limb. But I will prevail; I must prevail... *for him.*"

By the time Mrs. Grayson departed—after having related a seemingly endless story about how the glover's shop on the high street had closed its doors, and why the bulk of Marlhurst society chose not to patronize the draper who had opened in its place—Emma felt herself in need of a moment's quiet in which to collect herself. She begged her leave and stole upstairs to her dressing room, where her first thought was to gauge the toll the afternoon had taken on her appearance. She was amazed to find herself yet looking rather well. She felt as though she had been dragged five miles behind a galloping stallion; but there was no sign of weariness or abuse in her aspect. Even so, she did not know how much longer she could stave off the disfiguring effects of eroding hope.

She sat in the window seat overlooking the drive; and though she knew that no carriage would appear so long as she kept vigil—"A watched pot never boils," she had often heard her mother say (though how her mother would know such a thing was uncertain)—she could not seem to look away.

It was unthinkable that the Willmots should not come today. They were particular friends of the Marlows—Mr. Willmot and Sir Godfrey had even been known to enjoy a day's shooting together—and despite living outside Marlhurst proper, they were indispensable to the village's society. Where *were* they? Where was *he*?

She would have liked a confidant at this moment, to whom she might unburden her heart; but she had none. Frances was in many ways a dear sister to her—she had happy memories of their frolics and games when they were children, and even now they shared moments of merry fellowship—but Frances was entirely too self-contained to be in sympathy with any other human being. Emma could not quite regard this as a defect; it was simply Frances. Impossible to imagine her any other way.

Her Aunt Curtis might have served; she was certainly sympathetic—indeed, *earnestly* sympathetic; she solicited confidences the way a beggar solicits coin—but she tended to talk as much as she listened. And also—there was no use attempting to deny it—her understanding was not quite all it should be. Emma could not be certain that she would sufficiently grasp the fullness of the regard in which she held Edgar.

Edgar and Emma

But this was all beside the point, because Aunt Curtis was not at hand. She was to come later in the afternoon, and stay for dinner—by which time Emma would no longer require her compassion, because she would have seen Edgar. Would she not? She must. It defied all reason that the Willmots should stay away the *entire day*.

Her doleful thoughts were interrupted by a knock at the door. She said, "Come in," and was surprised to see Tom enter.

"I did not like the way you left us just now," he said. "You seemed in distress. Is all not well?"

And she found herself, to her surprise, confessing all to him. She had so persuaded herself of the need of a confidant, that his mere appearance at this moment had elected him.

"So you see," she said at the end of her oration, "what wretchedness it is to wait for him to arrive. All my hopes for the future are dependent on his coming today. I am suspended in agony until he does."

She now looked up at Tom, ready for what advice he might offer her; but in an instant she saw that she must be disappointed. He appeared utterly confounded; and really, she might have known it. He was like a brother to her; they had grown up together; and she had never known him to be easy with the vagaries of human feeling. He preferred the clearly defined precepts of the law. Were there a statute maintaining that the Willmots *must* come today or be fined for dereliction of duty, he would be able to reassure her; but as their nonappearance was a matter of simple caprice, he could not.

But then his face brightened, and she could not understand why until she saw that he looked not at her, but past her—over her shoulder and out the window. And when she turned to see what had delighted him so, she espied—could it be?—a covered carriage in the drive, with the Willmot's own driver (whose long, fishlike face she recognized at once) at the reins.

Oh, untrammeled happiness! She and Tom gathered at the casement to watch as the carriage disgorged its occupants.

First came Mr. Willmot, who after stepping out turned and extended his hand to his wife—who certainly required his aid, as she was so large that her balance on the step was not a thing anyone could depend on.

After she had been brought safely to ground, the eldest Willmot daughter, Patience, emerged; she looked much as she did when Emma had last seen her. Then came the two junior girls—the twins; very greatly changed indeed, but they had been the merest children when Emma had known them. Likewise Peter, the youngest Willmot, who now leapt out, bypassing the step altogether; he had gained a full six inches in the time the Marlows had been away. After which David issued forth, more handsome and broad-shouldered than Emma remembered him.

And then…no one.

Emma had been slowly apprehending, with each new Willmot who materialized, that the carriage was not large enough to accommodate *all* of their number; for they were, she recalled, some dozen or so in total. But it had not yet occurred to her that Edgar would be among those unaccounted for.

"Why does he not come out?" Emma said, concerned that he had perhaps suffered an injury that limited his ability to move without assistance.

It was not until the driver shut the door, climbed back into his seat, and with a flick of the reins drove the carriage out of sight, that she realized the full horror of the situation.

"He...he is not with them," she muttered, feeling as though the floor might give way beneath her. "They have come...but they have come *without* him." She looked up at Tom. "Whatever shall I do?"

He appeared less uncertain than he had before. "You will do what custom dictates," he said—but not unkindly. "You will do what you must." And with an encouraging smile, he gave her his arm. He seemed to understand—as Emma was beginning to—that one could stave off private dismay by observing the mandates of public duty. Her heart was crushed, her future barren; but she owed it to her father and mother to behave otherwise. She must represent them and do them credit.

She took Tom's arm, and let him lead her back downstairs.

"Ah! Here is Miss Emma Marlow at last," cried Mrs. Willmot when Emma and Tom reentered the parlour. "I would know her anywhere. My dear, you have quite blossomed; like something from a painting. Is she not like something from a painting, Mr. Willmot?"

"I beg your pardon, my dear," said her husband, who had been in private conference with Sir Godfrey near to the fire.

"I said, is not Miss Emma Marlow like something from a painting?"

Mr. Willmot gave Emma a cursory glance, then said, "Very like." And with that he turned back to Sir Godfrey and continued speaking in a low voice.

"And Mister Tom!" cried Mrs. Willmot. "Look, children," she said, turning to her brood, who sat ranged around her, "here is Miss Emma Marlow, whom many of you may be too young to remember; and with her is Mr. Peake, whom we had the pleasure of seeing just last summer."

The children dutifully conveyed their how-d'you-do's, and Mrs. Willmot smiled brightly at Tom. "I know you are soon to return to Cambridge. How long are we to have you to ourselves?"

"Not long, I'm afraid," he said. "Three days hence I depart to resume my studies."

"Ah! Well, then, we must make the most of what time we have. Sit, sit. I was just telling Lady Marlow the shocking history of our glover, Mr. Leonard. You will never guess—he inherited a fortune!"

As Emma took a place on the sofa, her mother gave her a very pointed look, which she understood to mean that she should not undermine Mrs. Willmot's evident pleasure in relating this story, by revealing that they had just heard it from Mrs. Grayson.

"Thirty thousand pounds," Mrs. Willmot continued, "from an elderly cousin he had never even met. I fear it quite went to his head. He decided that he was above remaining in trade, so he closed his shop. Mr. Harris, the clothier on Drake Street, made him an offer for it, but he wouldn't be bothered to consider it. He just shut his doors —left his inventory and fixtures and all, exactly as they were! And what do you think he did then, but take a house in town, and try to wriggle his way into society! I declare I do not know who he had advising him; but whoever it was, he did him no service.

"You can perhaps guess the result. His wife, silly by nature and overawed by her change in fortune, was induced to run away with the son of an earl. Which I daresay is not the way Mr. Leonard had hoped for his family to ingratiate itself with society. But I should not speak of such things in front of the children. Peter, David, girls—stop up your ears."

"Can we go and see the dogs?" pleaded Peter, who had much rather visit the spaniels (which Frances had removed to the kennel) than be privy to any tiresome grown-up scandal.

"We shan't be here long enough to make it worth your while. Just sit still and mind your manners. And you, dear Tom—do sit down! There is more yet to tell."

Tom had been performing a rather delicate maneuver— feigning interest in Mrs. Willmot's narrative while inching away from the group of women and children, and closer to Mr. Willmot and Sir Godfrey, whose conversation he must naturally prefer. But now Mrs. Willmot had fixed him in place—he could not without discourtesy refuse her—so with merely the slightest sigh of defeat, he lowered himself onto the settee next to Patience, who appeared only too happy to share it with him.

"After his disgrace," Mrs. Willmot continued in a lower voice, as though to prevent the children from hearing— though they could not possibly have done otherwise than apprehend every word—"Mr. Leonard wrote to Mr. Harris, offering him the shop for the same terms originally proposed; but by that time Mr. Harris had made an alternate arrangement, and so declined it. In the end Mr. Leonard sold out to a draper, a Frenchwoman named Mrs. Claude, except she insists that everyone call her *Madame* Claude, which is very difficult for English tongues, you know." It was certainly difficult for *her* English tongue, as each time she pronounced it, her jaw widened like that of an adder preparing to swallow an egg. "All was well for a time, until the day last Christmas when *Madame* Claude sold Mrs. Heath a bolt of muslin for two pounds-fourpence, but when the bill came it was for guineas, not pounds. Mrs. Heath brought the bill to the shop and pointed out the discrepancy, but *Madame* Claude refused to admit any error, and said it was the price agreed. Now it is not a large difference, but Mrs. Heath resented that she should be ill-used for even a few shillings, and refused to pay more than the original price *Madame* Claude had quoted, but the obstinate woman would take nothing but the amount she had billed. And it was too late for Mrs. Heath to return the fabric, for she had already had it made into a very smart morning dress, plus a cravat for her husband got up from the leftovers. So it was quite a stalemate, and remains so to this day. But I daresay *Madame* Claude regrets her meanness over those two shillings, because we who are friends of Mrs. Heath—and who have never known her to tell an untruth in forty years—have refused to patronize her since. And let me tell you what is most interesting in all this …"

Emma, whose attention had been waning, now stopped listening entirely. She had only managed to pay heed up to now in the vain hope that somewhere, in some aside or digression, Mrs. Willmot might make mention of her eldest son; but it was clear that she was no more to be diverted from her chronicle than a cannonball from its target.

Emma cast her gaze from one Willmot child to the next, in the hope of seeing some reflection of Edgar in their faces; but beyond the jutting chin common to all the Willmot progeny, she found very little. Possibly David resembled him most, because at fifteen he was on the cusp of manhood. But in truth—how dispiriting to realize it!— she had half-forgotten what Edgar looked like. The broad strokes of his features were still bright her memory; but the nuances—the curve of his nose, the precise set of his brow—eluded her.

She sat in glum silence, pondering this betrayal of her own recall until at length she heard Mrs. Willmot say, "We have taken enough of your time, Lady Marlow; I daresay other friends will soon come to call, and they will not like to find us here as well. Lucy-Anne, ring the bell to summon the driver, there's a good girl."

Again on impulse, Emma leapt to her feet and took a position before the string, effectively blocking it from anyone's reach. Lucy-Anne stood before her, perplexed; everyone else stared at her as well.

"Mrs. Willmot," she said—again marveling at the sound of her own voice, so free was she from any power over it—"you do not stir from this house till you let me know how all the rest of your family do."

Mrs. Willmot and her husband shared a meaningful glance; Lady Marlow and Sir Godfrey did likewise, and even Tom's and Patience's eyes met in mutual inquiry. But this was all in the space of a heartbeat; then Mrs. Willmot, in apparent good humor, undertook to answer her.

"Our children are all extremely well, my dear; but at present many of them are from home. Amy is with my sister Clayton; Richard is at Eton; Edgar at Oxford; and Ralph on an errand in town. I am very sensible to the honor you do me in asking after them. I hope to reacquaint you with them—or at least *one* of them—very soon."

She had such a twinkling in her eye when she said this, that Emma must blush—had her secret been guessed? Was she found out?

Yet none of that truly mattered…Edgar was at Oxford. She had feared him married, but it was almost as bad; he had become an academic. She ought to have known, by the scholarly turn of his mind, that he would steer himself that way. He was perhaps by now a fellow, or even a don, with lodgings on campus from which he would never again stir to return to humble Marlhurst.

After the Willmots departed, Sir Godfrey sought out his errant daughter to rebuke her for her rudeness to Mrs. Willmot; but Emma had already fled in tears, back up to her room, with the intention—blurted to Tom, whom she passed on her way to the stairs—of remaining there the rest of her life.

CHAPTER SEVEN

"Well, there's a good thing," said Mrs. Willmot as the family rode home. "All of them looking so well, and such hospitality! No one more welcoming than the Marlows; have I not always said so, Mr. Willmot? You'd never know five years had gone by. Except, of course, the girls so grown up."

"And Tom," said Patience. "Tom too; very much grown up."

"Yes, my pet; but we saw him not a year ago, so we knew that already, didn't we?" Mrs. Willmot shifted her weight to make herself more comfortable; she had Peter on her lap, the better to accommodate all seven of them in the carriage; but Peter was no longer of a size to fit any lap anywhere—a fact both he and his mother were loath to admit, though she less so every time they trundled awkwardly over a rise or gully, and his sharp hip bone bit into her midsection. "Though I must say," she continued, once she had adjusted herself into an easier pose, "that was an extraordinary outburst by Miss Emma Marlow, near the end. I don't mind saying, I felt myself quite challenged, indeed I did."

"Headstrong girl," said her husband with a harrumph. "I remember *her* well enough. That sister, too. Never forget the time they accosted me on the high street and all but extorted sixpence from me to buy sweets. Brazen, is what I call them." Too late, he remembered what had enabled the extortion in question—Frances and Emma having caught him sharing a furtive kiss with a shop girl behind the stationer's—but fortunately his wife was congenitally incurious, and did not interrogate him on the subject.

"I don't think Emma meant any discourtesy," said Patience. "It's just that she wanted news of Edgar, and hadn't had any; she had been patient, but wasn't willing to let you depart without any word of him."

"I daresay you're right, my dear," said Mrs. Willmot, as she again rearranged herself beneath Peter's weight. "Except that is it Ralph, not Edgar, of whom she craved news."

Patience shook her head. "No; I am certain it is Edgar. She has quite doted on him ever since he rescued her from that viper."

"It was a mere grass snake," said her mother; "he told me so himself. And yes, she was grateful to him, I recall it now. But I have it on the very best authority that Miss Emma Marlow pines only for our Ralph. Not," she added, with a smile of maternal pride, "that she would be the first."

Patience looked perplexed. "Are you certain? I suppose I may be misremembering. But I could have sworn her heart belonged to Edgar."

"Never mind, my dear. A young girl's fancy is a fickle thing; it alters with the wind...unless the gentleman in question chooses to fix it in place." She gave her husband a meaningful glance. "And that is our Ralph's specialty."

"A bit too much so, from all I hear," grumbled Mr. Willmot. "What the devil is the matter with this road? I don't recall it being quite so bad as this. Did we just run over a body?"

Edgar and Emma

"*You* were most attentive to Tom," said Mrs. Willmot, turning again to her eldest daughter. "That was very kind. He must *want* kindness, poor orphan, having lost his first family, and now divided from his second by university."

"I expect he will return for Christmas," said Patience with a hitch of desperation in her voice.

"No doubt, my pet; but remember, the Marlows always pass the Yuletide in Wiltshire. So we shan't benefit from his rejoining them."

Patience looked suddenly stricken, and turned her face to the window.

"Damnable thing, a university education," said Mr. Willmot. "Glad I never had one. Gives a young man all sorts of airs and fancies…Say, what was that about Edgar being at Oxford? Didn't you say he'd gone to Boars Hill, to see Amy and your sister Clayton?"

"Yes, my love," said Mrs. Willmot. "But that was just a stop on his way; his principal object was his old college, and his former mentor, Professor Bridge."

"But the boy's been graduated two years now! Why on earth would he want to run back to see any of those old black crows?"

"He has explained it often enough," said Mrs. Willmot, an edge of crossness to her voice. "Why do you never listen? Edgar has it in mind to be a scholar, and his old professor is advising him."

Mr. Willmot looked as though someone had struck him in the face with a day-old trout. "A 'scholar,' you say?… And what exactly would *that* entail?"

"Why, he's only told us a dozen times," said Mrs. Willmot with a great show of indignation, to cover the fact that she couldn't quite remember herself.

"I'm sure I'd have heard him, if ever he'd said something so damnably foolish," Mr. Willmot insisted, and his wife covered Peter's ears against any further strong language. "The idea! Edgar is my eldest son, my heir. His place is at Willmot Lodge, learning to be a country squire so that he may run our estates and manage our properties as I have done, and my father before me, and my father's father, and all the fathers before that, back six hundred years to when Sir Kennard Willmot was granted title to our lands by King John."

"That's as may be," said Mrs. Willmot, cautiously unstopping Peter's ears (to the boy's immense relief). "But Edgar has a quickness of mind greater than any our family has yet produced, and we owe it to him to allow it free rein. There is no telling how he may distinguish himself—and us."

"There is no telling," said Mr. Willmot sharply, "who will administer our affairs after I am gone, if he is off somewhere lying on a couch in a dressing gown, writing poetry in Greek."

Mrs. Willmot felt her face burn. "There is always Ralph. Ralph wants an occupation; you have said so yourself."

He waved his hand in dismissal. "Ralph could not administer a pot to boil."

Mrs. Willmot briefly reddened, for Ralph was her favourite, and she disliked any word said against him. "How would you know it, Mr. Willmot, as you have not tried him?"

"I know it," replied her husband, "as he has tried *me*."

And so the argument gained in amplitude and acrimony; and Patience, who under ordinary circumstances would by now have interposed some calming word to assuage her parents' tempers and lead them gently back to accord, did no such thing, because she was consumed by her own private grief, and insensible to anyone else's. Not her mother's; not her father's…

…and not Peter's, even when the boy muttered audibly, during one of the frostier intervals of silence that punctuated his parents' quarrel, "We really *might* have gone to see the kennel. It wasn't so *very* far from the house as all that."

CHAPTER EIGHT

As soon as Mr. Willmot was back at the lodge, he wrote to his eldest son and bade him return without delay. Then he went to make peace with his wife, of whom he could once again think kindly now that he had satisfied himself through the exertion of his paternal authority.

As it happened, Ralph Willmot had by this same time grown bored with London—his "errand" there having consisted of no more than a chain of louche amusements, of which he was now feeling more than surfeited—and had written to Edgar as well, to propose himself in Oxford. He surmised that the soothing torpidity of an academic environment might help him recuperate from the effects of his many indulgences; but alas, Edgar wrote back to say that he had been summoned home.

Ralph was disappointed; he had intended to delay his own return to Willmot Lodge by visiting his brother. But since it was not to be, he thought they might as well make the last leg of the journey together. They arranged to meet at The Copper Fox, an inn in Surrey much frequented by travelers from Sussex, there to eat and drink together before continuing on their way.

Ralph was the first to arrive, riding up in the pummeling heat of early afternoon. Once inside the cool, low-ceilinged common room, he took the opportunity to order a tankard of ale to quench his thirst. Indeed he might have time for another before Edgar turned up; which thought so pleased him that he wished his brother in no hurry. For despite the vast differences in their characters, the two young men were close, and each had an improving effect on the other: Ralph was not quite so comfortable debauching himself with Edgar's eye upon him, and Edgar was actually known to laugh in Ralph's company—there were eyewitnesses to the phenomenon who had reputably reported it.

After he had quaffed his first few mouthfuls, Ralph felt sufficiently recovered from the oppressive warmth to survey the other patrons in the room. He fully expected to discover a face familiar to him—but was surprised by the one which finally answered this expectation.

"Peake!" he exclaimed, after departing his own table and coming to where his old friend sat. "What a welcome thing, to find you here. You won't mind my joining you?"

Tom, who had been very happily passing the time with a book, none the less closed it and smiled agreeably. "Not at all. Hello, Willmot."

"So it's true," said Ralph, after sitting down and stealing another swallow of ale. "If you're here at the Fox, you must be headed north; which can only mean the Marlows are again installed at Graftings."

"I left them this morning," Tom said. "You knew, then, of our coming?"

"The excellent Mrs. Curtis told me of it, before I departed for town—from whence I now return."

"Ah, yes. She is not one to keep such a thing secret."

"A secret of any kind would kill her," Ralph agreed; "it would be a stone in her breast."

Tom smiled; but he would not laugh at his aunt. It would be ungenerous.

Ralph, however, was not troubled by such scruples. "She is like my mother," he continued, leaning back in his chair, very happy to have an audience. "They are both of them so very verbose. My brother and I have an ongoing game, whenever those two ladies find themselves in one room: we observe to see which dominates the conversation. The result is always the same: whichever manages to speak the first syllable. Because the other will have lost her chance, and there will never be adequate pause thereafter for her to leap in and claim the field."

Tom arched one eyebrow. "I can believe that is a game of *yours*; I am less persuaded that it is also your brother's."

"Oh, Edgar is more satirical than anybody knows. It just requires bringing out in him."

Tom nodded, while thinking, "What he means is, it just requires a bad influence."

"Perhaps I can demonstrate," Ralph continued. "He is to meet me here forthwith. He comes down from Oxford, where he is engaged in some tiresome project involving Greek texts. He has described it to me, but I never listen on principle."

"I will be sorry to miss him," Tom said, while producing a few coins from his vest pocket and setting them on the table, "but alas, I must again brave the heat of the day."

"You are headed to town?"

"Yes; but only to pass through." He gave forth with another wry grin. "My destination is Cambridge. I am a university man myself these days, and Michaelmas term begins shortly."

Ralph blanched. "I am sorry; I hope you will not mind my having spoken slightingly of academia."

"Not at all. The scholar's lot is not for every man."

"Are you reading Classics, like Edgar?"

Edgar and Emma

"No; Law, at Jesus College. I am in my second year. It seems Mrs. Curtis did not tell you *that*."

"Indeed she did not. Damn the woman."

At this unexpected irreverence, Tom laughed himself, as much from shock as from diversion; and suddenly he understood how Ralph's roguish charm might indeed crack his brother's virtuous veneer.

He recovered in an instant and got to his feet. "I am glad we met, Willmot; I may not be back at Graftings for some months, and would have regretted missing you."

"But you won't regret missing Edgar?" Ralph asked, a mocking glint in his eye. "Never mind, you cannot fool me: I know it is because you are a Cambridge man and he an Oxfordian. You are rivals, and must soon come to blows."

Tom laughed again. "I should think neither your brother nor I had much to fear from any blows such meek souls as we might land on one another."

Ralph walked him to the door. "There is something else Mrs. Curtis neglected to tell me," he said, "and that is how the Misses Marlow do. I have not seen them since they were the merest girls. They are well?"

"Both very well indeed."

"And...well-looking?" He gave Tom so pointed a look that Tom astonished himself by laughing a third time.

"My dear Willmot," he said, "they are as sisters to me."

"Very comely sisters, I expect."

"Since you ask, I believe they are generally considered quite handsome."

Ralph grinned in satisfaction, then clapped him on the back. "Safe travels to you, my friend. Be most attentive to your studies; graduate with honors, and take your place at the forefront of your profession. I do not wish this purely in a spirit of altruism, but from knowing that someday I am very likely to require a good lawyer."

As Tom rode north, he repented of the haste with which he had left Ralph's company. It wasn't due to Ralph's infamous conversation—for Ralph's easy charisma overrode any objection there.

No, it had been because he really *hadn't* wished to meet Edgar. Ralph had been more intuitive than he knew: indeed, Tom had no compelling desire to sit and compare notes with an Oxford alumnus.

Now, back under the punishing sun, his principles wilted in the unseasonable September calidity, and he felt increasingly ashamed that he had chosen not to meet a friend of many years over so slight a thing as a school rivalry.

He felt particularly regretful when he recalled Emma's fondness for Edgar, which had been the cause of so much recent misery to her. Tom might have waited to meet him, if only to advise him to treat her kindly. That this had not even occurred to him he now viewed with great self-rebuke.

He resolved to redeem himself by stopping in town long enough to post a short letter to Emma, informing her that Edgar Willmot was in fact on his way back to Marlhurst.

Edgar reached The Copper Fox some twenty minutes later, and after embracing his brother sat down with him and feasted on cold meats with bread and butter. While they ate, Edgar explained the reason for his summons home: "Father wishes to groom me to take over for him when he is dead. I would that I were not the eldest son, because I have no feeling for such things; I am a scholar, not a farmer."

Edgar and Emma

"Well, don't attempt to shift the burden of responsibility onto *me*," Ralph said (he had by this time finished his second tankard of ale). "You may be ill-suited to the role of country squire, but I think I must be its very antithesis."

Edgar smiled. "I had considered proposing such a thing, but abandoned it for the very reason you cite. David, however, seems to possess the kind of character that would exult in overseeing our estates."

"David is not yet sixteen. You perhaps read too much into his avidity for nature." He pronounced the word "nature" as though it burned his tongue to say it.

"No, I have watched him; he has a feeling for the soil, and for the animals. It brings something out in him. He seems in deep accord with it all." He sighed. "I very nearly envy him that. It is a kind of gift."

"Well, then! Will you nominate him to Father?"

"Not yet. As you say, he is very young. Let him first discover what other endeavors he might undertake, and if he still finds as much felicity in land management as he does now, he and I will conspire to make it so. And then I will be free to pursue my own ambitions."

"About which I pray you will not discourse at present," Ralph said heavily. "I am already rather weary."

Later, as they rode south, Edgar said, "You ought to give your own future more deliberation, brother. As the second son, you have the luxury of choice; I cannot adequately convey to you how fortunate you are in that."

Ralph rolled his eyes. "You speak as if my choices were legion; in reality, there is the church, there is the law, and there is government. Nothing else is entirely respectable for a gentleman. Alas, I find all three tiresome in the extreme. No, the thing for me is to wed some young lady sufficiently high in the social order to excuse her husband from any obligation of employment whatsoever." He grinned. "That said, what an excellent time for the Marlow girls to re-enter our lives!"

Edgar shot him a startled glance. "The Marlows? In what sense do you mean 're-enter'?"

"They have moved back to Graftings. Had you not heard? No, I suppose you wouldn't have; you must pluck your nose out of your books from time to time, Edgar, and listen to the word on the wind."

"The entire family, you say? Sir Godfrey and Lady Marlow, and both daughters?" He had tried not to expose himself, but the way he pitched that word "both" would have revealed him to anyone more mindful than his self-regarding sibling.

"The lot of them," said Ralph. "And Tom Peake as well; though he's now off to Cambridge. He was at The Fox just before you. Did I not mention it?"

"Indeed you did not."

They reached an expanse of road that was shaded by poplar trees, and slowed their mounts so that they might longer enjoy the comparative coolness.

"The Misses Marlow were pretty young girls, as you may recall," Ralph continued, taking the opportunity to produce his handkerchief and mop his brow. "Peake assures me that their charms have only increased."

"Tom Peake said that?"

"Well…I asked, and he didn't deny it." He looked contemplative as he tucked the kerchief back into his breast pocket. "I suppose either one would do, for my purposes, each being the daughter of a baronet. Though I seem to recall the elder sister running wild with something like a wolf pack."

Edgar and Emma

"I should've thought a thing like that might appeal to you," quipped Edgar.

Ralph gave him an astonished look. "Was that a satirical remark? Was it? Did Mr. Edgar Willmot, Oxford scholar and latter-day Cato, just utter a word in jest?"

Edgar laughed; but his brother's affectionate mockery was not the chief cause of his merriment. That, rather, was the certain knowledge that he would soon meet again a young girl who had frolicked at the periphery of his vision for years before he finally noticed her; a lovely, sylvan sprite whom he had once memorably—indeed unforgettably—carried in his arms.

CHAPTER NINE

"Today I speak to you of selflessness. Of all the virtues impressed on us by our Creator, none is so great as Christian charity. The early practitioners of our faith were not renowned for their forbearance, or for their chastity, or for their rectitude, although in fact these were essential to them; no, what set them apart was their duty to others. The first Christians distinguished themselves by their attentions to those in want; even they who were in want themselves, put aside their own needs and sought instead to comfort and serve the sick and indigent among their communities and their countrymen."

Mr. Nesmith paused; he would not have called it a theatrical moment—indeed he would have been shocked to hear it called such—but this was its effect. He looked down from his lectern at his visibly awed congregation, and continued: "But we latter-day unworthies, in our pomp and finery, congratulate ourselves on our righteousness based solely on the achievement of every seventh day coming to fill these pews, and tamping down for a single hour the rampant greed and self-interest that drive us like stallions the remainder of the week. We feast at the poison trough of gossip; we prey on the weaknesses of our brethren as vultures feast on carrion; we gorge ourselves on sweetmeats while others starve, and slake our thirsts with wine and spirits that dull our moral senses and set loose our basest demons. We cloy ourselves with excess, sicken our souls with our animal cravings, debase our flesh by giving free rein to our appetites, and in all ways reduce ourselves to cringing, chattering avatars of darkness. We serve no one— ourselves least of all—none but he for whom the fall of human honor is the tireless labor of many millennia. Even now he laughs at our self-delusions and hypocrisies, as we mire ourselves ever deeper in the black tar-pit of sin."

He lowered his head for a moment; then looked up and resumed. "As a final note, let us welcome back to our flock Sir Godfrey and Lady Marlow and their many fine children. May they prosper among us, and add to our share of blessings. Now rise, and lift your voices in Hymn number two-hundred-and-forty, 'O perfect love, all human thought transcending'."

The Willmots, by reason of their being the most ancient family in the neighborhood, were the first to exit the church, and thus to pay their compliments to Mr. Nesmith. Ralph in particular shook his hand and said, "What a stirring sermon! One finds one cannot wait to curtail one's gorging and slaking."

Mr. Nesmith—perhaps alone of all who lived—was not beguiled by Ralph's impudent charm. "Enjoy your levity while you may, sir," he said. "Rakehells never profit."

"Do you not think so?" said Ralph before moving on. "I fear you have been speaking to the wrong rakehells."

The Marlows, because of their exalted rank, emerged next, and Lady Marlow especially commended the parson on his address. "I am glad to see you have not lost your fervor, parson," she said, fanning herself slightly as though recovering from a not unpleasant ordeal.

"Nor never shall," he reassured her.

Mrs. Curtis skirted behind Lady Marlow during this exchange, averting her eyes from Mr. Nesmith; and once on the portico, summoned her husband to follow her to their barouche—a summons he was only too pleased to answer, as he had no use for the social talk on the churchyard green that followed every service. On an average Sunday his wife would be in the thick of it; but today she was strangely uneasy, and felt it imperative that she avoid the parson's notice. Were she a woman capable of even the simplest feat of reflection, she might have determined that this was because she feared his censure of those who fed at "the poison trough of gossip" had been aimed squarely at her. As it was, the vague inkling of having somehow put a foot wrong was enough to pull her from any company; though she was not so chastened as to go away entirely, and instead sat with her husband inside the barouche, observing what transpired on the lawn for later analysis.

Had she but known it, she was safe from Mr. Nesmith's scrutiny. Indeed she might have come right up under his chin and stood on his shoes, and still not managed to engage his notice. He was preoccupied with watching, from the corner of his eye, the progress of Ralph Willmot. He could still not rest easy that his daughter's dalliance with that young rascal had indeed concluded; for the term of their flirtation had forced father and daughter into their most steadfast opposition yet. He had insisted that she give him up; she had defied him, and threatened elopement if he pressed his paternal authority. So fierce was she in her defense of the attachment, that he could not but be mystified by how easily she then set Ralph Willmot aside mere weeks later. He had never dared to question her about it, lest he provoke her into renewing the connection; but he continued to watch her—to watch them both—for any sign that such a thing might be forthcoming.

Yet today Ralph did no more than bow to Alice before moving on to speak with the Lynches, who stood at some distance from her. Even more gratifyingly, Mr. Nesmith espied another young man approach and engage Alice in conversation—that being his verger, Mr. Redmond; a humble young man, but of excellent character and a cheerful disposition. He could not fathom what Redmond saw in his restless, unpredictable daughter, but whatever it was, he meant to promote it in any way he could.

As it happened, he was not the only one who at that moment regarded Alice and Mr. Redmond; for Edgar, too, caught sight of the couple just as they struck up their conversation. They seemed very friendly, which came as a surprise, because until very recently Alice had been rather obvious about her interest in Edgar himself. But then she had also once been equally forthright in her attentions to Ralph. Edgar found her agreeable enough, but suspected she did not quite know who—or what—she wanted, and was loath to become enmeshed in her experiments to find out.

Alice *had* been rather cooler toward him just before he departed for Oxford; could it be that her father's verger had by then engaged her interest? He dared to hope so; for he could not in good conscience give her any encouragement on his own behalf.

She must have sensed his eyes on her, because she turned and met them with her own; and by the smile that lit her face, Edgar knew at once that she had not replaced him with anyone else. Alas, he was still the principal object of her attraction. In fact she now dismissed the verger so curtly, leaving him almost in mid-sentence to come and speak to Edgar instead, that the poor young man was visibly startled; his jaw hung so low and so long on his chest, a bird might have made a nest among his molars.

Edgar cursed himself for his stupidity in spying on her, for now he had drawn her to him, and she was very much not the young lady to whom he wished at this moment to speak. But he could not turn and flee her, as she had done to the verger; his own manners were too correct for such discourtesy. And so he held his ground.

But before Alice could reach him, he felt a presence at his side, and turned—

—and there she was: the very person in all the world he most wished for.

"I beg your pardon," Emma said with pleasing demureness, "but I wonder if you remember me, Mr. Willmot."

"Indeed I do," he said. "And I hope you have had the good sense, these past few years, to steer clear of vipers."

She laughed very prettily. "Oh! it was not a viper; you said so yourself. Only a grass snake. I think you must mean to aggrandize your heroism, Mr. Willmot, by putting me in greater danger than I actually was."

He feigned an expression of great injury. "I am found out!" he exclaimed. But then he smiled and added, "I see that you have grown in wit, as you have in beauty."

She blushed. "You are too kind, sir."

"Not at all. I saw you within, you know; and had you not been seated with your mother and father, it would have taken me more than a moment to place you. The five years since last we met have done you many kindnesses."

She laughed again. "Was I so much to be pitied as that?"

"Not at all; I only mean you were then a bud, and now a blossom."

Edgar and Emma

Her face flushed anew; and he could sense that, behind him, Alice had halted in her progress toward him, no doubt having seen him become otherwise engaged. He felt free to suggest a stroll about the churchyard, and Emma, to his delight, agreed to the scheme.

"My father's ward, Tom Peake, writes to me that you are newly returned from Oxford," she said as they ambled away from the others.

He raised an eyebrow. "I was not aware that I was of such interest to him."

She colored again; Edgar enjoyed the sight. He wondered how often he might induce her to repeat it.

"You are no longer a student there, I think?" she asked.

He shook his head; and as the morning was proving rather warm for a walk, they stopped as if by mutual consent beneath a willow tree, to rest for a moment in its deep pool of shade.

"I am not," he confirmed. "But there is a lecturer there —Professor Bridge—who has become a mentor to me, and who is guiding me through a literary project I have undertaken."

"Indeed?" she said, and she looked at him with what seemed unfeigned interest. "And what is the nature of this project?"

"I'm afraid you would find it very dull," he said, remembering the glaze that had come over Alice's eyes when he expounded upon it to her.

"You think me a silly creature, then? Lacking in understanding?" There was an accusatory note in her voice that made him suddenly wary.

"Not at all," he said, gently taking her elbow and leading her back out onto the green. "Merely that it is a ponderous subject for so light a morning." She seemed to be considering this, and so to distract her he said, "Your sister looks uncommonly fine as well; for that was her, I believe, seated next to you in your family's pew. Does she still have her dogs?"

"Oh, Frances will never abandon her spaniels." She gave him a hopeful look. "And what of your own loyal friend? How fares my second rescuer, Pompey?"

Edgar softened his features so as not to appear too blunt. "He lived to a venerable old age and died in his sleep. I can wish no better for any of us."

Despite his efforts, Emma seemed distressed by the news. "Oh, but I remember him being so full of life, bounding alongside you! Surely five years are not sufficient to see such a vital creature into his dotage."

"Regrettably, their lives are set to a different tempo than our own."

This seemed to sadden her; perhaps she was thinking of her sister's dogs, and what just a few more years might bring. But then she surprised him by rounding on him and saying, "You have yet to answer my question."

He was quite confounded. "What question was that?"

"The nature of your literary project."

There was something about her manner...she was a delicate, slender thing, but there was iron in her; it showed in her carriage. She would not back down. He surprised himself by finding this enchanting; and so he relented.

"I have undertaken a new translation of Plutarch's *Lives*," he explained. "You are perhaps familiar with the work?"

She shook her head in the negative, but did not seem abashed.

"It is a series of parallel biographies, written in Greek, by the ancient historian Lucius Mestrius Plutarchus—or

Plutarch, as he is known to us." He scanned her face for any sign of regret that she had introduced the subject; but her eyes were bright and avid. "Each set of biographies pairs a noble Greek hero or statesman with a Roman who is his rough equivalent."

"Ah," she said, but with no languor in her tone; rather, she seemed to be urging him to go on. Which he took haste to do, as they had now made the circuit of the churchyard and were again approaching the other congregants—or rather, those who had not yet dispersed.

"For example," he said, "Plutarch pairs his biography of Alexander with that of Julius Caesar; and by this means, he allows the similarities and differences between them to illuminate their characters in a way treating them singly would not."

"How very clever," she said; and though he listened for mockery in the words, he found none.

Thus emboldened, he felt able to confess to her something he had told no one else—excepting of course Professor Bridge. "The reason I have chosen to make an English translation of my own," he said breathlessly, "is that I have a plan to enlarge the work; and that is by—"

He was interrupted by the sudden appearance of his mother. Given her girth, Mrs. Willmot was not known for sprinting across churchyard lawns, so her sudden arrival by his side rather startled him; indeed, he lost his hat.

As he stooped to retrieve it, his mother said, "My dear Miss Emma, I am so glad to see you have reacquainted yourself with my Edgar. Did he know you, I wonder? I would not be surprised if at first he did not know you. But I have another son just returned, as well; and I think you must not play favourites. That would never do. You will of course remember Ralph. He is just there, under the window of the nave, speaking to Mr. Grayson. Will you do me the courtesy of saying good morning to him? I will be happy to lead the way."

Emma could not but agree; and as she turned to go she gave Edgar a guileless smile that almost made up for her being taken from him.

Except that while Emma went on ahead, Mrs. Willmot hung briefly back and said, "I am sorry to be so brusque, Edgar; but you will forgive me when you understand me better. It seems that Miss Emma Marlow is very taken with our Ralph, and being a young lady of excellent breeding is too shy to approach him. So as his mother I take it upon myself to bring the two lovers together. There! now I hope I am forgiven." She happily turned away from him and made after Emma, who had paused to look back, in apparent curiosity at her delay.

Edgar watched his mother lead Emma to where Ralph —now alerted to their coming—had stepped away from Mr. Grayson; and continued to observe as Ralph bowed to Emma, and even kissed her hand, as was his wont, while Mrs. Willmot gabbled happily on.

It was only a few moments before Edgar became aware that he now stood in no less stupefied a state than the verger had, when abandoned by Alice. He shook his head, and with a great summoning of self-command pulled himself back to order.

And yet he was still astounded. Emma Marlow...in love with *Ralph*?

But then, why not? All the world was in love with Ralph. Edgar himself adored him, for all his failings. Ralph had the means to make it so; he boasted good looks, and courtliness, and an uncanny charisma that could draw the birds down from the trees. In love with Ralph?...When the alternative was dour, scholarly Edgar and his tiresome Greeks and Romans, who would be otherwise?

As if in answer to his question, Alice drew up beside him. Had she been following him at a distance, while he and Emma walked the entire churchyard 'round? Perhaps so; and while five minutes before the idea would have alarmed him, now he found a measure of solace in it. Alice, at least—who knew Ralph as well as anybody—seemed to prefer Edgar's company.

Alice, and Alice alone.

Well, then, he ought not to punish her for such partiality. He offered her a smile and said, "I have just been speaking to Miss Emma Marlow."

"I have seen as much," she said; and if there was a serrated edge of jealousy to her words, what of it? In his present state, Edgar could not but see it as a tribute.

"She is much changed," he said. "You are of an age, I think."

"We are neither of us yet nineteen," she said, as if affirming that Emma had not *that* advantage of her and daring him to try another.

He was happy at this evidence that she cared enough to campaign for him. He extended his elbow. "You must not stand beneath the cruel sun," he said. "I would not have you wilt; I would have you flourish."

She beamed at him, and took his arm, and he led her under the roof of the porch, where they stood and talked until Mrs. Willmot called him to come to the carriage. When he looked up, he saw that all the other families had since gone, and he had not been aware of it.

He had not even noticed Emma Marlow depart.

CHAPTER TEN

Emma, dismayed that she had not been able to catch Edgar's attention before leaving the churchyard—and even more distraught that the impediment to doing so was his apparent fascination with Alice Nesmith—again took to her room with the stated intention of shutting herself up for the rest of her days. She enjoyed having this stratagem once again available to her, after the barren months in Chipping-Norton; but she was also becoming reacquainted with the difficulty, after the gesture had been magnificently carried out, of reneging on it when it subsequently became inconvenient.

Self-incarceration, she was remembering now, had not suited her. After the Willmots' visit had prompted her to resume the tactic, she had swiftly grown bored with herself and weary of her grief, and maintained her isolation only out of dread of the embarrassment she should face if she ended it so soon. But when Tom's letter had arrived, alerting her to Edgar's imminent arrival, she joyed at her deliverance; for the reason for her seclusion no longer applied.

But there was little chance of that now. After she had wept out the initial ravages of her disappointment, she lay on her pillow and rationally examined the possibility of another face-saving miracle. It was slight. She could scarcely expect providence to come to her aid a second time; and even if she could, what might that aid consist of? A letter advising her that Alice Nesmith had been struck by lightning? She could not in good conscience wish for it, little as she cared for Alice—and the two had never been on good terms; not since they were very young, when, having grown tired and irritable over a game they had been playing for far too long, they had fallen out over the rules. Each one invented a regulation that favored her over her competitor; each then accused the other of trickery, and neither admitted the deceit; with the result that Alice had pulled Emma's hair, and Emma had pushed Alice into a cow-pat. They were forced by their fathers to make it up; but each was strong-willed and nurtured a secret strain of rebellion in her breast, that kept them at arm's length from that day to this. They might be coerced into civility, but they would never again choose to be friends.

It sometimes seemed absurd that the effects of a petty childhood falling-out should yet be felt in full adulthood; but Emma could think of no possible amendment of it now. Except, in her less guarded moments...Alice Nesmith being struck by lightning.

At six o'clock she was called to dinner, as though no-one were aware of her intention to emerge nevermore from her room, though her mother and father and sister had all clearly heard her declare it as she fled up the stairs. It was a mark of their disrespect of her feelings that they simply assumed her anguished determination was no more than a pose, easily enough forsaken. She half fancied showing them the real strength of her resolve, by adding a campaign of fasting to her isolation...

...And yet she *was* rather hungry, and foregoing food altogether would only amplify, not mitigate, the terrible boredom of being shut up here; and so she concluded, reluctantly, that a parental summons was reason enough to set aside her vow of self-exile, and come downstairs and join the others at table.

As it happened she was safe from any gloating comment at her expense; for this very thing had happened often enough that it was, to her family, entirely unremarkable.

It was fortunate that Emma had ended her lifelong confinement in this manner, because the following morning Mrs. Curtis came to Graftings to beg her company on a series of errands which it would be excessively tedious to have to attend to on her own. It would have been tiresome for Emma to have to refuse her because she was yet maintaining fidelity to her tragic vow.

As she dressed for the outing, she scolded herself for having got herself into the same predicament twice in the space of a week, and vowed to better suppress her more operatic impulses, that they carried more weight on the rare occasions she chose to employ them. Since these two recent bouts had been prompted by extremes of grief having to do with Edgar Willmot, she felt it might be best to avoid him entirely; for should she happen again to espy him doting on Alice, she could not depend on her reason.

Alas, she might conceivably evade him in the flesh; but the *idea* of Edgar was not so easily skirted. She learned as much within her first five minutes out-of-doors. She had known, of course, that the reason Mrs. Curtis sought her company was that she wished to talk—there being no circumstance in all of Creation in which Mrs. Curtis would not wish to talk—but she had not suspected that today, what she wished principally to talk of was the male Willmots.

"You turned the heads of both brothers on Sunday," she said as they headed toward the high street, arm in arm. "Mr.

Edgar and Emma

Curtis and I could not but notice it. That is to say, I noticed it and I pointed it out to him, and he did not contradict me. But I think I can guess which of the two pleased you best."

"I hope you will not make the attempt," said Emma, with no small dread.

"In fairness, I do think their finer qualities are evenly distributed; do not you? Edgar is very much the responsible one; his is the cooler head, his the sounder judgment. He possesses a very comforting gravity, and an endearing trustworthiness." Mrs. Curtis recited all this as if describing a very well-made suit of clothes which she never wished to wear.

"Whereas Ralph," she continued, "is the more suave, the more charming, the more conversationally adept. He is also more certain to be delightful company, and to notice everything, and to frame it in such a way as to make one laugh. Do you not agree?"

"I cannot *dis*agree," said Emma carefully.

"But while their characters are thus balanced, I think there is, alas, less equivalence in their aspects. Edgar is very self-contained and very graceful; but he has not the same advantage of countenance as does Ralph. Surely you will concur. Ralph is by any measure the handsomer of the brothers."

Again, Emma could not argue the point; but she would not give her aunt the satisfaction of saying so. Mrs. Curtis placed far more importance on appearance than she did; and Emma would not encourage her by confirming a judgment based on such superficial terms...though she knew her aunt would press the matter. If only something would occur to divert her attention!

At just that moment such a thing did occur; but not in a manner which Emma would have wished. For at the juncture where the high street met the road to the parsonage, they were intercepted by Alice Nesmith.

Mrs. Curtis was delighted. "Come and join us, dear Alice!" she exclaimed. "We are headed for the shops—as I deduce, by the basket on your arm, you are as well."

Alice looked for a moment like she might turn and run; then she steeled herself, came forth, and fell into step with them.

"Good day to you, Miss Nesmith," said Emma.

"And to you, Miss Emma Marlow," said Alice crisply. "I congratulate you on your return to Marlhurst."

"Oh, have you not yet renewed your acquaintance?" Mrs. Curtis asked. "What luck to have run into you then, Alice; for we are just now having a very illuminating tête-a-tête. What do you think Emma has just been telling me of?"

"I am sorry to confess," replied Alice with perhaps too much satisfaction, "that I have not heard Miss Emma Marlow speak sufficiently often to guess at what she might say."

"Why, she has only been saying which of the Willmot brothers she finds the most handsome. I think you may surmise which she chose."

"I beg your pardon, Aunt," said Emma, feeling color come to her face. "I have said not one word on the subject. The discourse has been entirely your own."

"But there are so many Willmots," said Alice, ignoring Emma's protest; "I don't like to venture a guess as to which one you mean." But her eyes—which she now turned on Emma—betrayed that she had indeed ventured a guess.

"Difficult creature," said Mrs. Curtis, and she playfully tweaked Alice's arm—a familiarity that made Emma feel quite faint. "Why will you never guess when I ask it of you?"

Edgar and Emma

"I am sorry, but I am very stupid at it."

"I will have to tell you, then," said the older woman, and she drew Alice closer that she might lower her voice. "It is of course Ralph whom Emma favors."

"Aunt," Emma cried, "forgive me, but I never said such a thing! It was yourself that named him."

By this time they had reached the shops and joined with other villagers who were out with their baskets, running their errands in the relative cool of morning, before the inevitable heat of midday.

"Ralph is very fair," said Alice with a nod of approval. "Though I confess I prefer a darker complexion. No doubt Miss Emma Marlow and I have not the same taste in men."

Emma, who did not like to consider that she and Alice Nesmith might have the same taste in anything, stilled the protest that was poised to leap from her tongue; in which interval her aunt renewed her discourse on the male Willmots.

"That is the benefit, you see," she said, taking Alice in one arm and Emma in the other and leading them up the street, "of having so very many brothers in a single family. There is certain to be one to fit every fancy. Think of it, girls: Ralph is light, Edgar is dark; Richard is slender, David is burly; and Peter—well, Peter is too young yet to say what he will be. I suppose we must be content to wait."

"I think he will be tall," said Alice. "He is very high already, for just twelve years."

"Then the Willmots must be persuaded to have another son," quipped Mrs. Curtis, "that there may also be one who is short."

"But what if he should instead be round? Then the Willmots must have yet two more sons: one who is short, and another who is gaunt."

"Mrs. Willmot will not thank you for that, my dear," said Mrs. Curtis, and the two laughed very wildly. Emma, whose elbow was securely interlocked with that of her aunt, could think of no greater mortification than to be seen with them behaving thusly, and indeed several heads turned in response to the noise they were making. But alas, she was to learn that greater mortification always awaits those helpless to defend against it.

"Why, bless me," cried Aunt Curtis, "are those not two of the gentlemen we have only just named?"

Emma looked up, and to her dismay saw that indeed Edgar and Ralph Willmot were a short distance ahead, very near to the milliner's shop.

"Emma, my dear," said Mrs. Curtis with telling deliberation, "was not our principle destination this morning the milliner's?"

"No, indeed, Aunt," said Emma, pretending not to take her meaning, "we have no business to transact there."

Mrs. Curtis gave her arm a little shake. "Silly creature! You understand me, I am sure. I mean to say, what a chance this is to speak extemporaneously to your lover, Mr. Ralph Willmot!"

Emma felt her face burn again. "I have no such lover," she insisted.

"Ah, but here is an opportunity to make it so!"

"The mere fact that an opportunity presents itself," Emma said desperately, "does not signify that it is advisable to take it."

Mrs. Curtis cawed out a laugh. "How clever you are! Ever ready with a turn of phrase. I suppose you think that gentlemen find cleverness an attractive quality in a lady. They do not. You may trust me on this, my dear; I know it for a certainty."

Edgar and Emma

"I am sure no one knows it better," snapped Emma; and as soon as she had said it, she regretted that provocation had rendered her impertinent.

Fortunately her aunt was oblivious to her meaning, and merrily pulled her in the direction of the milliner's shop.

"I declare," said Mrs. Curtis when they came within hailing distance of the brothers, "here are friends of ours! Look, girls; it is the Misters Willmot."

The brothers, who had been conferring together, raised their heads at this, and a momentary look passed between Emma and Edgar—a look of such candid, unaffected interest that each was embarrassed by it, certain that it must be misconstrued—after which they turned their glances quickly away, and did not risk allowing their eyes to meet a second time.

"How do you do, ladies," Ralph said as he and Edgar tipped their hats.

"Very well, thank you," said Mrs. Curtis. "We are just come to visit the milliner's. And what," she added with unconcealed glee, "do you think we have all been talking of?"

Emma, whose skin was so recently reddened by shame, now felt it go pale with horror. "Aunt, no," she whispered.

"You must not ask us to guess," said Ralph. "For we might scandalize you by deducing quite wrongly."

"Then I will have to tell you," said Mrs. Curtis, and as Emma felt herself begin to sink into the ground, she declared: "We have been singing the praises of this lovely weather."

"Indeed it is very clement," murmured Edgar, whose gaze remained downcast, as though in search of coins from Roman Britain that might easily be unearthed by the toe of his shoe.

"Such a wonderful moistness in the air," said Mrs. Curtis with a quick glance at Emma; and the spark in her eye revealed how much she enjoyed causing her niece trepidation, then relieving it at the last possible moment. "So beneficial for the skin. Does not Emma's visage have a particular glow this morning, Mr. Willmot?"

"Indeed it does," said Ralph, at whom she had quite pointedly directed the question; for Edgar seemed to drift ever further to the outskirts of the group. "And yet she looks no less fine than Miss Nesmith—or I daresay yourself, ma'am."

Mrs. Curtis laughed wildly again. "You must not say such things, Mr. Willmot! I am an old married lady."

He flashed her a dazzling grin. "Then this moist air is more efficacious than any I have yet known; for you look no less a maiden than your two companions."

Again she shrieked with laughter; up and down the street heads turned in curiosity at such stridency, and Emma longed to be away from them. But she knew she was fixed in place for the time being. It was unlike her aunt to hurry from a place where compliments were in plenty.

"To be sure," Mrs. Curtis said, "there is but a difference of seven years between my niece and myself. My brother Marlow is fully fifteen years my senior, you know; so that I was but a child myself when Emma was born."

"That explains it," said Ralph with another bow. "I congratulate your husband, ma'am, on his good fortune in securing so young and comely a bride."

"As well you might," she said with a little smirk of pride. "For Mr. Curtis was nearly forty when I married him and might have done much worse, as I often tell him. But I daresay I have made him happy. He will not say so; but as he has not got rid of me in all these years, I must conclude he is not unsatisfied."

"He is the happiest of men, I am certain," said Ralph.

She crowed again. "Oh! if Mr. Curtis is the happiest of men, then what dour creatures all the rest of you must be!" She turned again to Emma. "I shall wish better for my niece, sir; that I shall. For her, I shall wish a husband who is always gallant, always gay, always ready with a compliment." She took another quick look at Ralph, as if requiring further inspiration, then added, "A well-looking fellow, who is always considerate and obliging. *That* is my ideal. *That* is what I wish for Emma."

"Such a paragon as that!" said Ralph, shaking his head and feigning a dubious look. "I wonder whether he exists in the world."

"I am certain he does. In fact, *you* may be sure there is one to be found wherever you go." She gave him a very sly look, as if daring him to take her meaning.

"Aunt," Emma whispered frantically; "you grow too bold."

"And Miss Nesmith," Ralph said, nodding his head at Alice; "is she not included in your marital good wishes?"

"Oh, I shouldn't like a cheerful husband," protested Alice. "I should be much more contented with a sober-minded man—a scholarly man of great, mindful silences." She did not look at Edgar as she said this; but Emma saw Edgar's color deepen, and he turned further away, as though he felt Alice's eyes on him all the same.

"Then at least," said Ralph, "you ladies will never be rivals for the same suitor. I congratulate you on the safety of your friendship." He turned his head, as if to say something to Edgar, then appeared momentarily confounded at finding him so far off. "It appears my brother is impatient to depart," he said, "and indeed we have lingered here longer than we had ought. But with such company as this, none would dare to blame us."

"Such gallant words have bought you your release," said Mrs. Curtis, waving him away. "Go, then; we will detain you no longer."

As soon as the brothers were beyond the range of hearing, she turned to Emma and squeezed her forearm. "Did that not go well? How attentive he was! How rhapsodic in praise of your fine skin!"

"I believe," said Emma, "he meant to praise each of our complexions in equal measure."

"Oh, foolish girl; that was but a blind! He included Alice and me the better to mask his compliment to *you*."

Emma looked at her with incredulity. Was it possible Mrs. Curtis really believed what she said? When Emma had last known her, she had admired her aunt very much, and thought her the pinnacle of all womanly achievement: a beautiful young wife with a fine house and a liberal husband who allowed her to do as she pleased. Now that Emma had reached womanhood herself, Mrs. Curtis appeared very differently to her; she seemed to be rather the younger of the two, as if her early marriage had frozen her in a perpetual state of juvenile giddiness. Were her aunt now to pick up her skirts and turn a somersault in the high street, Emma would be embarrassed, but not surprised.

"I must bid you good morning as well," said Alice. "I begin my rounds just ahead, at the tobacconist's, as my father has once again let his pouch go empty."

Emma was surprised to hear a daughter speak so sardonically of a parent; she kept her counsel, but the incident did nothing to inspire her to think better of her former friend.

Edgar and Emma

Thus Alice left them, buffeted by Mrs. Curtis's regretful effusions; after which aunt and niece went on alone. Emma had to endure another four minutes' dissection of their encounter with Ralph, until by chance they passed the draper's shop, and Mrs. Curtis must abandon all talk of the Willmots and tell Emma the shocking history of Madame Claude. Emma, grateful to be quit of the earlier subject, listened to the narrative with great equanimity, though she had already heard it twice before.

Thus at the end of the morning, each of its principal participants returned home secure in an entirely erroneous conviction.

Ralph was certain, by the way Mrs. Curtis had spoken, and by the way Emma had blushed at it, that his way to the latter's heart was clear.

Edgar was equally certain of his brother's success with Emma; and was additionally persuaded, having now seen both girls together, that Alice suited him much the worse of the two—but that she was, all the same, the best for which he could hope.

Emma was surer than ever that she could not be in the presence of Edgar and Alice without suffering great unhappiness. Never mind that he had behaved diffidently towards Alice; it was clear Alice had not minded it—which, to Emma, meant that she had accustomed herself to such behavior from him, and did not find it an impediment to love.

Mrs. Curtis was confident that she should soon triumph on two separate fronts. Her campaign to match Emma with Ralph Willmot gave every indication of success; and by the way Alice spoke of preferring "a scholarly man of great, mindful silences," it was clear she was indeed an ideal match for Tom Peake, did she but know it—and Mrs. Curtis would see that she did know it.

As for Alice herself…she was the least deluded of those here enumerated. For she was certain that Emma was less immediate a danger to her than she had feared, and that she had somehow gained an advantage with Edgar—an advantage she meant to press.

And let the consequences be what they may.

CHAPTER ELEVEN

"I see that once again I intrude upon your reading," said Ralph as he sat down, crossed his leg, and rakishly propped his hat upon his knee. "I seem always to find you with your nose in a book. And unless I am mistaken, it is the *same* book. It must be a very long one."

"It is lengthy," Emma admitted, politely closing the cover—but keeping her hand inserted into the pages, to imply that she expected this interruption to be but a brief one.

"Might I know what it is about?" Ralph said, jiggling his foot so that his hat danced upon his knee, like a character in a Punch and Judy show.

"It is *The Countess of Montgomery's Urania*, and it is a romance of the last century concerning a queen and an emperor."

"Ah! So it is a love story. As I would expect, for so genteel a reader as yourself."

"It is chiefly a love story, but there are many hundreds of characters, and many and varied incidents of all kinds."

He let his jiggling foot droop. "It sounds tiresome in the extreme. Very like life itself. The fellow who wrote it must not have lived much in the world, if he felt compelled to recreate it in the pages of a book."

"Its author is Lady Mary Wroth."

"A woman! Well, that explains it, then. Also the length. Are not women known for their ability to go on and on? Make no denial; I've heard you do it."

As he wagged a teasing finger at her, Emma felt herself begin to color; yet she forced a serene smile onto her face. Her chief desire at this moment was to flee Ralph Willmot, to run upstairs and shut herself in her room for the rest of her life. But as she had recently availed herself of that maneuver not once but twice, she felt she had better not overdo it.

In addition, she knew it would only encourage Ralph. He would see her distaste for him as a challenge. If she showed him that he had some power over her, he would strive to reshape that power into the form he desired. So rather than present him with a tempting bulwark of opposition, she treated him instead with polite indifference. That, she knew, was the way to put him off.

"You are very disdainful of our sex," she said with what she hoped seemed idle curiosity. "It is a wonder, then, that you so often choose to place yourself in our company."

"Ah," he said, raising his hand in testimony, "but you have other charms that more than recompense your constant chattering."

"I am glad you think so," she said, pretending to stifle a yawn.

A moment passed; then he said, "Are you not curious as to what those other charms might be?"

"No, indeed. Were I to ask, you would consider that I was begging for flattery, and you would despise me for it."

He smiled in triumph. "And you would not have me despise you?"

She adopted a look of surprise. "I would have no one despise me. Certainly that is true of anyone. What, is it not true of you?"

"I would have the rascals and japes of the world despise me."

"I would have the rascals and japes of the world not know me," she said airily. "But then I am, as you observe, not a creature of the world. Perhaps it is easier for me to avoid such persons. Though not," she said, making a point of quietly moving her chair back a quarter-inch, "entirely."

She saw a look of irritation play across his face, and felt once again the full measure of her powers. He had called on her several times this past week, which alone signaled his interest in her; but she had stymied him every time by countering his attentions with a show of blithe detachment. Surely he must soon tire of having no effect on her, and give up the effort.

In the meantime she must forebear. Consistency of tone was her strongest weapon. In the strictest sense, propriety ought to have come to her aid by obliging her mother and sister to sit with her when Ralph Willmot called; but given that she and Ralph had known each other since childhood, it seemed to Lady Marlow no serious breach to leave them alone. They had, after all, been so many times in the past. And as for Frances—

—Well, that thought was answered in the present moment, as a cacophony of barks and growls filtered through the sitting-room windows.

"Your sister is exercising her spaniels, I take it," said Ralph.

Emma shrugged. "That is a given at any moment of the day. But in the present instance, she is additionally hosting Mr. Denham and his Labrador." She attempted to put on a long-suffering aspect. "He is as frequent a caller as your-self." The implication, she hoped, was that he was here *too* often.

"Ah!" he said, thwarting her by seizing the opportunity to use this comparison to suggest that similar motives were at work. "And may I, from that, conclude an attachment between them?"

Emma did not need to feign shock at this. "Certainly not! Mr. Denham is past fifty. He is the senior by a decade of my own father."

He gave her a sly look. "The heart cares little for such distinctions."

She felt her color rise again. "They have made common cause of their love for dogs, that is all; and he is advising her on the renovation of our kennels. I assure you, there is no more to it than that."

"I think you may be mistaken. In fact, I am certain of it."

She did her best to smile knowingly. "I am certain that I am right."

He smiled back, but there was mischief in his aspect. "Then given your certainty, would you consent to a wager on the matter?"

She lost her smile in the tumult of her astonishment. "Mr. Willmot, I am not one of your public-house cronies!"

He laughed, not at all abashed. "I would have you stake no coin, Miss Emma; I do not do you that indignity. I ask only that, should I be proven right in the matter of your sister and Mr. Denham, you acknowledge as much by ren-dering me a courtesy."

"What kind of courtesy?" she asked, suddenly wary.

He furrowed his brow. "I cannot say as yet. Perhaps it will be a painful one to you; but you must honor your commitment all the same. Unless," he said, giving her a sidelong look, with a maddeningly arched eyebrow, "you are not so sure of your assessment of your sister's friendship as you say. In which case, by all means, decline the wager."

She sensed that he was attempting to lead her into some kind of trap, and for a moment considered denying him the pleasure. But then she thought, "What of it? I know I am right about Frances, so naught will ever come of it."

"I accept your terms," she said with a nod.

He sat back in his chair, thoroughly pleased with himself. "Then I need do no more than anticipate the day, and the manner, in which I claim my due. And hope that you will learn from the experience."

She felt herself redden; this bordered on impertinence. "And what is it, pray tell, that you wish me to learn?"

"That sometimes there is great ardor and affection staring us square in the face, and yet we cannot—or will not—see it." His eyes fairly twinkled.

This was a dangerous moment; Emma knew her color was betraying her—but what it betrayed was merely heightened feeling. Ralph could not know that that feeling was not delicacy or endearment, but a panic at having inadvertently offered him encouragement.

She cleared her throat and said, "I forget my manners. I have not yet offered you refreshment." In fact, she had not offered him refreshment because she wished to maintain the surmise that his visit was to be of no more than a few moments' duration; but given that he appeared so settled, she gave up the dissimulation, removed her hand from its place in the book, and rang the silver bell at her side.

The parlour maid entered the room. "Miss?"

"Tea, please, Sarah."

The girl darted a look at Ralph from the corner of her eye; he returned it, and she departed in what seemed undue haste.

"You needn't go to any trouble on my account," he said, once it was too late to do anything about it.

"Nor need you on mine," she said, impertinence bubbling to the surface at last. "And yet, here we are."

At this point one might well ask why Emma was so steadfast in her resistance to Ralph Willmot; for his attractions were manifold, and while she had indeed been acquainted with him in childhood, she had not known him well enough to despise him now. It was rather a matter of the presence of Ralph always summoning the shade of Edgar—and shade he might as well be, for Emma received through Ralph regular confirmation of his pursuit of Alice Nesmith. But though Emma must content herself to have no sooner rediscov-ered Edgar than lost him, she was too proud to settle for second best—which is how she, and she alone, viewed the more obvious charms of Edgar's brother.

One might with equal justification ask why Ralph himself persisted; and for him it was a matter almost of intellectual curiosity. He might easily have abandoned Emma in favor of another rich man's daughter, if a life of wealth and ease were his sole consideration; but Emma's indifference to him intrigued him, for he had never encountered such a thing before. He must prod and poke and investigate it, and if possible overcome it; his ego demanded as much.

But the effort required could be wearying, and today he left Graftings very much vexed. He had paid court to Emma for more than a week and she had rewarded him by being barely cognizant of his presence, much less of his intentions. He might almost suspect her of feigning insensibility.

But he was certain it was more a matter of long acquaintance dulling the edge of attraction. And while it was true that they had not seen each other in five years, and that those five years had wrought changes in both that might be expected to atomize any sense of overfamiliarity (it was certainly true of him; he remembered her as a willful young girl—now she was an alluring young woman), there must be enough in him still of what Emma had been accustomed to seeing there, to turn their meetings, which ought to be thrillingly flirtatious, into what for her seemed the sheerest tedium.

Very well, then, perhaps it was time to take the opposite tack. If his presence was so inconsequential to her, might his absence be more keenly felt? He would go back to town and disport himself there, and let Miss Emma Marlow see how she liked a world suddenly deprived of his suavity and wit; perhaps he would be greeted with greater enthusiasm when he returned.

Edgar fared no better in his own romantic pursuits. Admittedly he undertook them with a somewhat fatalistic feeling; as we have noted, he would have preferred to pay address to Emma, but had become accustomed to see his brother do so in his stead—and with every apparent success. Whenever Ralph returned from having visited Graftings, Mrs. Willmot would inquire, "And how do you speed with Miss Emma, my dear?"—to which Ralph's reply inevitably took the form a broad grin, a wink, and a lunge at the family mastiff, Bravo, which initiated some good-natured rough-and-tumble. Such high spirits, Edgar deduced, must be the giddy manifestation of a deeply felt satisfaction.

And so he found himself occasionally visiting the parsonage, where Miss Nesmith never failed to strike exactly the right chord of welcome—expressing just enough joy at the sight of him to assure him that his continued attentions were yet very welcome, while at the same time sufficient ease of manner to convey that he need not stand on formality; that as far as she was concerned, the parsonage was his second home.

But he never *felt* at home there; and he wondered how anybody could, given the presence of Mr. Nesmith, whose demeanor at all times suggested he was on the point of issuing a verdict of guilty and pronouncing a sentence of death on the entire human species. "Rode over, did you, Willmot?" he would ask, in the same tone with which he would have asked, "Murdered your mother, did you, Willmot?" so that Edgar was sorely tempted to lie—but for the presence of his horse, tethered outside; and the suspicion that to have come on foot might be seen as even worse.

Mr. Nesmith acted as chaperone during his visits, but only in the loosest sense; for he sat at the desk in his office, whose door opened onto the parlour, in full sight of Edgar and Alice, and composed his sermon for the coming week, so deeply immersed in this work that he never as much as looked up; certainly he lost all cognizance of his daughter and her suitor in the adjacent room. Edgar and Alice, however, could scarcely be unaware of *him*, so that it was almost as though they were the ones charged with supervising *his* conduct; and if they ever managed to relax their vigilance to the point of forgetting him, he would recall himself to their attention by means of rehearsing a certain turn of phrase, in such abundant voice as frightened birds into flight from the tree beyond his window.

Edgar and Emma

Such an atmosphere was ill suited for wooing; and yet Alice rewarded Edgar's every attempt with limpid-eyed gratitude, as though they were alone together in a field of heather, under a starry sky.

Edgar was grateful for such encouragement, but also rather disheartened by it; for while he was glad to know that the sentiments he expressed brought pleasure, he had no urgent wish to amplify them. Alice was very pretty; Alice was very kind; Alice was patience itself, and deserved every happiness; but to say more than this seemed ostentatious.

Instead, he chose on this day to test the limits of the kindness and patience he so lauded. Ever since the day on the church green, when he had come almost to the point of revealing to Emma the true nature of his translation project—only to be interrupted by his mother—he had felt that he must tell *someone*. He had not known until that moment how much he wished for another human soul to share in his excitement; and if Emma could not be the one to gratify the longing she had inspired in him, he would try Alice instead.

"I have told you, I think, about my literary undertaking," he said.

"Have you?" she asked—and while it was deflating that she had forgotten it, it flattered him that she seemed keen to know it now.

"My translation," he began, parsing out the explanation in short bursts so as to allow her to stop him at any interval with an assurance of yes, of course, I do remember it now; "from the Greek—of Plutarch—his biographies—the *Lives of Noble Greeks and Romans*." Still she regarded him blankly, so he suppressed a defeated sigh and went on. "Well, perhaps I have not told you after all."

"I think I would have recalled it," she said. "It sounds so very interesting. And you will really render it into English, from the Greek?" She placed her hand over her breast as though unable to contain the sheer wonder this bred in her.

"Yes—though it has been done before," he said, "by the brothers Langhorne in the year 1770; but I mean not merely to improve on their edition, but to expand the work itself."

She wrinkled her brow. "I am not certain I apprehend your meaning."

"I mean," he said, his heart beating, "to add a third element to the work, by incorporating chapters on the lives of notable personages of our own great empire. So it shall be, under my hand, *Lives of the Noble Greeks, Romans and Britons.*"

She nodded very slowly; he could not tell whether he had bored her with this information or whether she was simply stunned by its magnitude and daring.

Neither, as it happened. "It seems to me a quantity of work," she said.

"Yes, but *what* work!" he enthused, moving closer to her on the divan. "I will be the first man of letters to make an explicit connection between the personages of the Classical peri—"

"Whore of Babylon, painted and pampered," howled Mr. Nesmith from the next room, *"wallowing in your wantonness, unbridled in your debauchery!"*

Edgar paused a moment, to allow for any further declamation; and when none came he continued. "I think I have told you—no, forgive me, we have established that I have not—but I will enlighten you now, that Plutarch's *Lives* is structured so that a short biography of a Greek luminary is paired with one of a Roman worthy with whom he shares certain defining qualities. And the juxtaposition of those biographies is meant to illuminate the men under observation, by highlighting both their similarities and—often more revealingly—their differences."

Alice nodded; yet he could not but notice that she began to play idly with the fringe on her skirt.

"My innovation," he continued, a bit falteringly, "will be to add a third point of comparison. So that, for instance, to the chapters comparing and contrasting Alexander and Julius Caesar, I will append a brief biography of our own empire's analog: our greatest general, Oliver Cromwell."

She nodded again, but the effort to listen was beginning to tell in her.

"The abutment will reveal much, I think; and to our advantage. For example, Alexander was the son of a king; Julius Caesar an aristocrat. Each, then, had the blood of warriors in his veins. But Cromwell was a man of the middle gentry; his success owed nothing to ancestry, and everything to his own native genius."

Alice scratched her cheek. "I see," she said. "And all this labor will avail you…what, I wonder? Do you anticipate a great publishing success?"

His shoulders slumped and his heart withered. "I would certainly welcome it; but it seems unlikely, and is well beside the point."

"Forgive me; it is the point that I have trouble comprehending."

Edgar considered how best to make her understand—a feat of reasoning made no easier by Mr. Nesmith roaring from the next room, *"Man is a beast in fancy dress, powdered and perfumed to contain the stink of corruption and the oozing of contagion"*—and eventually settled on the following:

"Learning requires no justification, Alice; it is inherently self-validating. The reward for attempting to understand our relationship to our ancient forebears is the endeavor itself. Honor, glory, financial remuneration—these are the things we come, by such undertakings, to value but lightly. They are ephemeral; they are fleeting; and in the grander scheme they mean nothing at all."

She appeared to contemplate this for a few moments; and Edgar waited with some anxiety for the response that might very well determine his future.

At length she smiled and said, "I take your meaning; and it is a very admirable one."

But her eyes had hardened, and her look was at odds with her tongue; so that when Edgar met her gaze, the message they conveyed was, "*You are wrong.*"

CHAPTER TWELVE

It was not long after Ralph had kissed his mother goodbye and ridden off to London that word came back that he had offered offense to someone in town—which was not without precedent—and had been challenged to provide satisfaction by means of pistols at dawn—which was a shocking innovation in Ralph's history.

Mrs. Willmot contrived to keep the news from her husband, and even from Patience—who she feared might betray the ill tidings to her father by means of a pale complexion or an inability to hold back tears. But she confided it to Mrs. Curtis, whom she knew to be fond of Ralph, so that she should have someone on hand to comfort her until word arrived of how the affair had concluded. And thus two days were passed in the most awful agitation, before a friend newly arrived from town delivered the welcome intelligence that the earlier report had been much exaggerated. Ralph had been drawn into a bout of fisticuffs which had left him bloodied but not broken; but there had been no suggestion of a duel—at least, not until the story, traveling south and gaining amplification along the way, reached the attention of a gifted raconteur in Croydon who had happily supplied this improving detail before passing it along to the next set of ears.

After the first transports of her relief had faded, Mrs. Willmot found herself yet unnerved by the experience. "For

I tell you, Mrs. Curtis, the ease with which I credited the account that so alarmed us is to me a warning that it might yet come to pass. It is the wonder of Ralph's nature that he inspires in others either the most abject devotion or the most avid detestation; fortunately the latter is the rarer phenomenon, but how much longer before such a thing turns mortal? I cannot bear to think on it; and yet I seem unable to think on anything else."

"The thing for Ralph," said Mrs. Curtis, patting her friend's hand consolingly, "is to be wed; a smart, sensible wife would put an end to his roving and curb his indulgences; and fatherhood would oblige him to set an example. He must marry, Mrs. Willmot, and soon."

"I am certain you are right, Mrs. Curtis," said the lady, daubing at her nose with an already damp handkerchief, so that her friend was moved to produce a fresh one to offer for her use; "thank you, most kind—as I say, you are certainly right. But how to manage it? He has on occasion taken an interest in a particular girl, only for that interest to wane—most recently, Miss Emma Marlow."

"I do not think my niece quite knows what she has let slip through her fingers," said Mrs. Curtis a bit crossly. "After the fuss she made over him on her return to Marlhurst, she ought really to have given him more encouragement."

"I daresay she is shy of him; and Ralph is not accustomed to timidity."

"Emma is not shy; she is, quite the contrary, rather willful and sometimes too forward. I think she must be toying with him; yes, I am persuaded of it. And yet she will not be told so; depend upon it, she will not hear it said."

Mrs. Willmot paused momentarily, with the new handkerchief pressed daintily against one nostril, and said, "Perhaps, if she is so *very* contrary, it is to Ralph's benefit that he has given her up."

Mrs. Curtis felt her face drain of blood; this was the opposite of what she had wished to convey. "Not to his benefit at all, Mrs. Willmot, if you will pardon me for saying so; only a woman who is willing to deal with Ralph on her own terms, as opposed to his, has any hope of restraining his impulsiveness. Emma is the one for him, you will see."

"Perhaps I shall, Mrs. Curtis; but will *he* see?"

"We must make him—you and I."

"And how will we devise to do so?"

Mrs. Curtis thought long and hard; during which interval Mrs. Willmot creditably soiled the fresh napkin (to such a degree that Mrs. Curtis found herself wishing never to have it returned) and tucked it up the sleeve of her dress, feeling moderately restored to equanimity.

"There must be a dance," said Mrs. Curtis at last. "Nothing promotes affection between the young quite like music and finery. It seems fully an age since the last one; and with the Misses Marlow back in residence, there can be no better excuse."

"And who will hold it, my dear? Willmot Lodge as you know is not up to the task"—which was true not by design (for the house had a very large and high-ceilinged room quite suitable to the purpose) but by circumstance (a case of dry rot had rendered the very room unadvisable for occupation, at least until repairs were effected)—"and as you have often observed, Mr. Curtis will never consent to such a party being held at Shakers."

This was only too true; though it hurt to be reminded of it, as Mrs. Curtis's fondest wish was to enjoy the glory of entertaining her friends in her own house.

"Sir Godfrey must be persuaded," she said. "Graftings, while small by a baronet's standard, is yet the grandest house after the Lodge; and it would be a handsome way of reintroducing the family to the neighborhood."

"That is perhaps so; but it would be rather bold of us to suggest it to him."

"You forget—he is my brother. I may take liberties with him that are denied to others."

Mrs. Willmot began to look hopeful. "I may leave it in your hands, then?"

Mrs. Curtis was on the point of assuring her friend that she might indeed do so; but they were interrupted by the housekeeper, who informed them in a rather distracted manner that the dog had eaten one of Peter's temporarily discarded shoes and was in some gastric distress, and that Peter himself was now inconsolable because he very much wanted the shoe back. Mrs. Willmot must quite literally rise to the occasion; and while she was hefting herself from her sopha, Mrs. Curtis made her excuses and slipped away.

In fact, Mrs. Curtis was not so confident of her influence over her brother as she had let on. She was, after all, fifteen years his junior and rather in awe of him; and while it suited her that Mrs. Willmot should think her on such comfortable terms with him that she might advise him to hold a dance at his house, she could think of nothing that would more thoroughly daunt her.

But she was on good terms with her brother's wife, and had known her long enough to know how to accomplish her errand through that avenue. She need only persuade Lady Marlow that the idea of a dance at Graftings was her own idea; which seemed a thing easily enough done.

Edgar and Emma

And it would be a thing well done, too; for not only was it imperative that Ralph and Emma be brought back together and inspired to be more mindful of each other, it was only slightly less urgent that Tom Peake should come home and initiate some claim on the parson's daughter. Alice Nesmith had, alarmingly, been receiving calls from Edgar Willmot, and with every appearance of satisfaction; if Tom did not step in soon, it might be too late for him; and Mrs. Curtis, knowing that Alice favored him, did not wish to see the poor girl settle for anyone less, simply because the gentleman in question had removed himself from any possibility of her company.

Accordingly, when Mrs. Curtis found herself seated in the drawing room at Graftings, with Hicks pouring tea for her and Lady Marlow looking very well disposed to have someone to talk to, Mrs. Curtis did not wait to launch her attack, but began as soon as the housekeeper had retreated and left them alone.

"My nieces are looking uncommonly handsome," she said, pausing only long enough to blow a cool breath across the surface of her tea before continuing. "I know I have said so before, but it continues to astonish me. They are so very altered—so graceful, so womanly! How I would enjoy seeing them dressed to best advantage—but absent a dinner party, or even better a dance, I suppose I shall have to content myself with imagining it."

"Alas, so it would seem," said Lady Marlow before sipping tentatively at her own steaming cup. "And may I say, you are looking very well yourself, my dear; your cheeks are full of color. I wish I could find it in me to walk with such regularity and spirit as you do. How far have you sojourned today?"

Ordinarily Mr. Curtis would be completely derailed by such a compliment; but her object today was too important to set aside for a mere promise of additional flattery. She tacked back into the wind: "I have only been to Willmot Lodge and back; a mere three miles. Poor Mrs. Willmot! I think she is lonely, so far out from the village. And she cannot entertain, you know, for her ballroom is in ill repair; otherwise she might enjoy such delightful society as would be afforded by hosting an occasional dance. But then, what lady would not find pleasure in such a project?"

Lady Marlow, who had seemingly imbibed her fill for the moment, set her cup and saucer on the table and said, "I cannot imagine how Mrs. Willmot manages to be lonely in a house brimming with children. I should think rather that *lack* of privacy were her chief complaint."

Mrs. Curtis, now twice deflected, felt a little sting of frustration in her forehead, but would not relent. She took another sip of tea, the better to strengthen her resolve, and said, "Yes, but her children are so unregulated and wild. If one is to enjoy one's progeny, I think, one must provide the proper setting for them—set them a clearly defined stage upon which they might be seen to best advantage. For example, a dance."

Lady Marlow nodded rather airily and said, "I find that I enjoy my own daughters in every setting; perhaps I am a better parent than I know. I hope that does not seem proud; but are not Frances and Emma fine girls?"

"Very fine, as I have only just said," Mrs. Curtis replied, rather more curtly than she had ought, but it annoyed her that she was having to repeat things she'd already proclaimed, while the meat of her message was still dangling, like bait on a hook. "Your pride in your daughters does you credit; I could only wish that there were some occasion at which you might witness the high opinion of others for them as well, as for instance, say, *a dance*."

Lady Marlow waved a hand in dismissal. "Oh, I care nothing for the good opinion of others."

"No indeed," said Mrs. Curtis, feeling the room grow rather warm as she flailed for a new means of insinuation. "Far better to think of giving of oneself, than of receiving things like empty acclamation. Far better, indeed, to be the means by which others experience joy, as in, for instance—*hosting—a—dance*." She underlined the phrase so definitively this time, that she was persuaded Lady Marlow could not but hear it.

And yet her hostess's reply was of the same character as its predecessors. "I am in complete agreement," she said. "Just two nights past, Sir Godfrey and I noted how gratifying it was that we were able to help the parson's campaign for a church organ by contributing seven pounds towards the cost. He was most appreciative."

And with that, Mrs. Curtis admitted defeat...but only for her plan of subterfuge and manipulation. Ever determined, she would not yield the field without, at the last, attempting a direct strike.

"Jemima," she said, resorting to the use of Lady Marlow's Christian name, which she had not much employed since the sunny days of the lady's engagement to her brother, "I think you and Godfrey ought to host a dance at Graftings, to reintroduce Frances and Emma to the young people of the village."

"Do you indeed?" said Lady Marlow, raising an eyebrow as if the idea were something entirely unexpected. "Why...I see your point, Amelia. What excellent counsel! And I daresay, we are very to likely enjoy it ourselves."

CHAPTER THIRTEEN

News of the Marlows' dance was greeted with delight by the denizens of Marlhurst, as it had been nearly two years since there had been anything similar. And the recollection of that occasion was a goad to Alice Nesmith's ambition, for at that time, she—just sixteen, and eager to embrace life in its fullness—had not been invited.

The reason given—which made its way to her through various channels and in apologetic whispers—was that the public rooms on Hayworth Street, which is where Mr. and Mrs. Treacher entertained the celebrants, were insufficiently large to accommodate more than nine couples; but Alice was certain that she had not been asked because she was not out.

She was determined that there would be no repetition of that slight; she would go to the Marlows' dance. She did not yet know how she would manage it; but no mountain would bar her way, no assembled army would keep her from the door of Graftings. *She would go.*

It was more than a matter of pride to her; it was also a matter of some urgency. It had been several days since Edgar had last called, and with each sunset she grew more certain that she had put a foot wrong—made some unforgivable gaffe that had made her less agreeable to him. She was fairly certain it had to do with the matter of his literary project; she had perhaps allowed her lack of enthusiasm for it to show in her demeanor. But it had been a hard thing to suppress; for in truth she had no sympathy for the endeavor, and did not intend that all her hard work in separating Edgar from his duties as master of Willmot Lodge should be in the service of him instead holing up in a library with a store of ink and a Greek vocabulary. No, her plan was that he should live in town—and she with him—and enjoy the wealth that came from his estates while leaving others to supervise their operation. And it were best he should be nudged in that direction now, so that when he finally inherited the title, she would have him ready.

But she had perhaps nudged too brusquely; she had, on reflection, better have begun by flattering the project, and then later, over a span of time, diminishing it by slight degrees—a dismissive word here, a pitiful observation there—until he were finally persuaded to see its inadequacy as an occupation for a gentleman of his stature.

The mistake might yet be amended; but only if she were able to regain Edgar's attention. And she did not know how she should manage that, save by attending the Marlows' dance, where he would be unable to avoid her.

So the matter was settled. She would go.

But how? She was, at eighteen, no more out than at sixteen, and given her father's obstinacy she would be no more so at fifty, or indeed ever; she wondered whether she would even be allowed Christian burial after her demise, or if it would be judged that Miss Nesmith could not rest among her co-religionists in the sweet serenity of the churchyard because alas, Miss Nesmith was not *out*.

This unhappy thought was prompted by Alice actually passing the small cemetery that lay behind the church; it was her regular route into the village, and she was so accustomed to it that she scarcely gave it a thought; but today, inspired by her self-pity, she tossed it a fleeting glance—and her eye was caught at once by movement therein.

She approached the low brick wall which bordered the yard and took a closer look, curious to see what could be responsible for animation in this place dedicated to stillness.

Ah! but it was only Mr. Redmond, exercising one of the more humbling duties of his office: that of gravedigger. He seemed hard at it, too; he had removed his coat and loosened his collar, and rolled up his sleeves that he might periodically mop his damp brow with his forearm.

Alice now felt a slight shiver of alarm, as she had not heard of any deaths in the village; and she wondered whether, when she got to the high street, she should be greeted by some dreadful news of a ghastly accident or a pitiful stillbirth. But then she recollected that old Mrs. Stanley, who had reached the epic age of ninety-seven, had been faring very ill, and was expected not to last beyond the end of the month. It seemed likely that the poor woman had finally succumbed.

She was about to step back and continue on her way, but found that there was something pleasurable about watching another person who is unaware of being observed. And there was also, she thought, something attractive about the sight of Mr. Redmond—usually so meek and reserved—engaged in so physical an undertaking. It prompted her to think rather differently of him than she had been used to.

And just like that, a plan formed in her head.

It had long been evident to her that Mr. Redmond liked her; that in fact he would gladly seek to woo her, should he ever manage to find the courage.

Edgar and Emma

But what if Alice made courage unnecessary by offering him an easier road? A few smiles and blushes might be all that were required, and an earnest (or at least earnestly expressed) interest in him and his history. Within days, he would be her slave in all things.

And from there it would be a simple matter to provide enough evidence of his devotion for the gossips of Marlhurst to begin speaking of an attachment between the parson's daughter and the verger, and even to wonder openly when an engagement might be announced.

And a girl who can be spoken of as attached, and in expectation of an engagement, *must* be considered out.

Even so, there was little time to spare. So—after looking in both directions, to assure herself that there was no one nearby to witness the shocking thing she was about to do— she clambered over the graveyard wall, then smoothed out her skirt, patted her hair back into shape, and made her way daintily between the gravestones to where Mr. Redmond— who now at last espied her—set by his shovel and stared at her in open-mouthed wonder.

Did Alice but know it, her plotting and scheming were entirely unnecessary. It was always Mrs. Curtis's intention that she attend the dance, because that is where she meant for Tom Peake to win her heart.

And it seemed that Mrs. Curtis's intentions held some weight in the matter. For, having enjoyed such success in conceiving and bringing about the dance, she and her friend, Mrs. Willmot, persuaded themselves that they might also dare to suggest a guest-list; that Lady Marlow might indeed even thank them for it.

They were hard at it now, in Mrs. Willmot's parlour, Mrs. Curtis actually holding a ledger in her lap, with a pen poised over it, ready to set down names or strike them through as the negotiation required. Alice Nesmith's had already been inscribed there—"For while it is true she is not out," Mrs. Curtis had said, "I think such distinctions need not worry so small society as ours," and Mrs. Willmot had yielded the point—and they had gone on to debating the merit of other village daughters.

"I do think," Mrs. Willmot said, "that we cannot suggest Miss Arabella Mason without also making a claim for the three Misses Pine, who are her cousins."

Mrs. Curtis disdained to add these names, instead wrinkling her nose at the idea. "But the Misses Pine are entirely unlike their charming kinswoman; they are all so very plain, and dance so ill; no gentlemen will ask them. And that great, honking laugh of theirs!—I am convinced it will perturb the orchestra."

It was at this juncture that Patience entered the room, her face adorned with a joyful smile. Her mother had sent her on an errand that had kept her away for several days, and she had only just this moment returned, clearly glad to be back home.

"Ah! my dearest daughter," Mrs. Willmot said, "come and sit beside me, and tell me how does my sister Clayton."

"Very well, Mama," said Patience, taking her usual stool near the corner of the room; "she sends her love, and so does Amy. How do you do, Mrs. Curtis?"

"Very well, thank you, Patience."

"She was glad of the return of the charger, I reckon?" Mrs. Willmot inquired.

"Very glad, Mama."

This was a reference to a very old brass charger, with silver trim, that had belonged to Mrs. Willmot's mother; Mrs. Willmot had always fancied it, but after their mother died it had gone to Mrs. Clayton instead. Mrs. Willmot had slyly waited some years before asking to borrow it; and once it was sent to her in genuine good will she had made up her mind to keep it forever. And so matters had stood for fourteen years, with Mrs. Clayton inquiring, with both increasing regularity and increasing asperity, when she might have it back again; and she might be asking still, had not Mrs. Willmot seized on the contested item as the best means of getting Patience out of the house, so that she would not hear of her brother Ralph's participation in a duel. Accordingly she had wrapped the charger, given it to the girl, and sent her by carriage to Boars Hill to return it—with instructions to stay a day or so longer than the errand required, the better to visit with her sister Amy, who was Mrs. Clayton's companion.

Patience had clearly enjoyed her stay, and Mrs. Willmot had certainly missed her; but seeing her again, she could not but regret the loss of the charger—especially since its sacrifice had been unnecessary, as Ralph had not, it turned out, been in a duel at all. Rather unjustly, she found herself now blaming Patience for the entire fiasco, and after the initial warmth of her welcome home she rather sulkily ignored the girl.

So that when Patience asked, "What is it that you and Mrs. Curtis are about, Mama?", it was left for Mrs. Curtis to reply, as Mrs. Willmot seemed intent on remaining silent.

"We are drawing up a suggested guest list for Lady Marlow," Mrs. Curtis said, turning to address Patience in her corner. "You have perhaps not yet heard that the Marlows are to host a dance at Graftings on the twenty-eighth?"

"I heard it at the stable as soon as I arrived," Patience said, taking up a tambour and resuming the embroidery she had set aside six days before. "It seems to be spoken of everywhere."

"Yes, and we are certain Lady Marlow must have much attendant business to occupy her; and since she has not been in the neighborhood for five years, we thought to do her this favor at least."

"That is very kind," said Patience, looking up long enough to smile.

Mrs. Curtis, gratified by having successfully framed her meddling as courtesy, turned back to her hostess. "We have given too much thought to the young ladies," she said. "What of the young gentlemen? Although," she added with a laugh, "what with your own five sons, and dear Tom Peake, there will be few enough spaces remain-ing."

Mrs. Willmot sniffed in dismissal. "Oh, my Peter is only twelve; he is too young to attend. And Richard is away at Eton; I do not think he need be recalled. For that matter, Tom Peake is only lately departed for Cambridge. I do not expect he will come."

"Oh, but he must!" Mrs. Curtis exclaimed.

"He must indeed!" Patience echoed, dropping her tambour into her lap. "Mama, Tom Peake must surely be invited!"

Both Mrs. Willmot and Mrs. Curtis were taken aback by this passionate declamation from the usually quite reticent Patience. It took a moment for Mrs. Willmot to manage a reply.

"He will certainly be invited," she said; "it is his foster-mother and father who are hosting the affair. I mean only to say that he will likely decline; he is not, I understand from Lady Marlow, very fond of social occasions and prefers not to dance, and will also likely be burdened by a plenitude of reading at his college. And you, my dear," she added, addressing Patience more directly, "I think must be yet excited by the novelty of your journey; you would do well to rest an hour or so before rejoining us."

Rebuked, Patience muttered an apology, set her tambour back down again, and left the room.

When she had gone, Mrs. Curtis said, "It's all very well, what you say about Tom Peake; but I will hold him a place on the list out of courtesy to the Marlows. And I think he may astonish you after all, Mrs. Willmot."

And what she was thinking, even then, was that she would see to it that he would do so. By hook or by crook— *he would come.*

CHAPTER FOURTEEN

It was an odd thing, thought Edgar, that of the many worthies who in Plutarch's view merited inclusion in his *Lives*, Lucius Quinctius Cincinnatus was not among them. Was there ever a nobler Roman? He served as consul, the republic's highest office, with great distinction; but he achieved his lasting fame after he had retired to his farm, having been driven out of public life by political foes. Twice he was recalled by the Senate to serve as dictator in an emergency; on both occasions he served for exactly as long as required by the crisis at hand (one a war with the Aequi tribe, the other a civic rebellion), then resigned the office and went back to plowing his fields.

Edgar tried to conjure the spirit of Cincinnatus as he was led about the Marlhurst holdings by his father and the estate manager, Mr. Shore, on a particularly torpid morning. It was possible, in his estimation, that Plutarch had not provided the great Roman statesman a biography in his work, because there was no Greek parallel—no Hellenic leader who demonstrated similar civic virtue by relinquishing the world of affairs to attend the nurturing of the earth. In which case, Edgar wondered whether he might strive at least to be Cincinnatus' British analog: a man who, in the name of duty, gave up the world of ideas to devote himself similarly to the ancient arts of tillage and husbandry.

Edgar and Emma

It was a handsome design, and he congratulated himself for having formed it; but as the morning wore on, he must admit it worked better as a conceit than as a conviction. Agriculture in the abstract might have a certain appeal; but its actuality was so complex, such an amalgam of facts and fancies, innovations and traditions, that there was no system one could master that would guide one through each new encounter. What was required instead was a lifetime's mastery of unrelated minutiae, absolutely daunting in its scope to any newcomer. Already this morning Edgar had been instructed on no fewer than four methods for the healing of a cow's split hoof, each one dependent on the size of the crack, whether it was afflicted by a fungus, or whether it oozed pus or liquid—in which further case the color and aroma of the discharge both signified.

He had begun, scandalously, to suspect that Cincinnatus' fealty for his farm was less a tribute to the bliss of tending it than to his having no other retreat once duty had done with him; and he thought it fair to ask whether, if the early republic had had anything resembling a library, Cincinnatus might have preferred to devote his declining years to its corridors.

In any case, the desired correspondence between the great Roman's fate and Edgar's own was on reflection even more absurd, because Edgar would be handling none of these duties himself. Not even Mr. Shore was obliged to show such firsthand commitment to the property under his care. No, all such chores were the province of the tenant farmers—the industrious yeomen who lived on, and worked, the plots apportioned them from the Willmots' lands. Edgar's main duties, when he inherited the estate from his father, would be limited to rents and relations—adjudicating disputes, looking after the health and well-being of his tenants, and the like. And he would have the living of Marlhurst in his gift as well; but Mr. Nesmith was a vigorous man of no more than eight-and-forty, so even that weighty matter seemed out of Edgar's hands until a future so distant it might as well not exist.

But it was his father's earnest belief that a gentleman farmer should understand farming, even if the validity of his title rested almost entirely in the modifier and not in the noun. Edgar attempted to argue to the point on logical and philosophical grounds, but Mr. Willmot was not receptive to logic or philosophy, to the point of reducing them to "folderol" and "malarkey."

"You desire an analogy, sir?" he challenged his son at one point. "You crave an example from your more exalted world of finery and foppery, that will illustrate the matter to you?—Very well. I have it for you: One does not, I daresay, manage the Dulwich Picture Gallery without understanding painting. Is it not so? Whether one paints oneself is beside the point; a proper curator must fathom its mysteries. He must grasp its particularities. Am I not correct, sir?—Come, I'll not rebuke you if you speak plainly. Have I not made my case?"

Mr. Willmot was being ingenuous; in fact he would have rebuked his son very thoroughly had he spoken plainly. But in point of fact Edgar was silenced not by this anxiety, but by the more abashing realization that his father had indeed made his case.

If that were not sufficiently mortifying, what came next supplied what was lacking. The three men rode up to the farmhouse occupied by a married couple, Mr. and Mrs. Hare, who had lived there for nigh on twenty years and who had a brace of children—at least one of whom was likely to continue on the premises after Mr. Hare died. At first it seemed, as they approached, that they were witnessing the tenant farmer training one of his sons for just that purpose, each banging away at a broken wheel, while the wagon from which it had been removed sat askew on the ground like a drunkard.

But when the two workers turned to greet the new arrivals, Edgar was stunned to see that Mr. Hare's helper was none of the farmer's own progeny—but Edgar's own brother, David.

"Hello, Father," David said, setting down his hammer.

"Good morning, Davey," said Mr. Willmot, his tone as merry as Edgar had ever heard it. "And to you as well, Hare. What are you about, here?"

"Mr. Cousins, the wheelwright, is down with the ague," said David happily. "But I wagered Mr. Hare we could repair his damaged wheel ourselves. I have often watched Mr. Cousins at work, and I am certain I can replicate his methods."

Edgar would not meet his father's eyes, but he felt them begging him to do so, so that they might convey by a look: *There, that is the spirit I speak of.*

Instead he waited until his father and Mr. Shore dismounted; then he did the same, and followed them as they toured Mr. Hare's parcel of land and were instructed in its current condition—including recent challenges, how these difficulties were met, and the resultant expected yields—which instruction came often as not from David as from Mr. Hare himself.

For Edgar, the rarefied world of Lucius Quinctius Cincinnatus seemed very, very far away.

It is, alas, the lot of women that while the minds of men may rove the world over, the minds of ladies are principally engaged by men. Many would not have it so; but until the world remakes itself in its entirety, so it will be. And thus it was that while Edgar mused on Cincinnatus, Emma mused on Edgar.

This unfortunate distraction may have been aided by Emma being the only member of her household who in the present moment had no occupation. Sir Godfrey rode out every morning, on what business none bothered to inquire; Lady Marlow was busy planning the coming dance with Mrs. Curtis (or perhaps more accurately, Lady Marlow was busy nodding her approval of the plans proposed by Mrs. Curtis); and Frances was in daily conference with Mr. Denham, who arrived just after breakfast and sometimes did not depart until nearly four. Emma often recalled Ralph Willmot's insistence that there was some understanding between these two, but still could not bring herself to credit it; romantic as she was, she could not make herself believe that even the tenderest hearts required as much time as Frances and Mr. Denham devoted to each other. Surely after so much continued exposure, Romeo would weary of Juliet, and Paolo seek relief from Francesca.

It was Ralph's absence that had rendered Emma victim to such idleness and introspection; for prior to his departure for London, he had been her only steady visitor. For this reason alone she might have thought of him more than fleetingly; but she had heard from her mother some news that had turned her mind quite definitively back to Edgar.

Alice Nesmith, it seemed, had formed an attachment with her father's verger. This had come as something of a surprise, because it was only a fortnight earlier that Edgar's attentions to her were the talk of the village. But now, it was said, Edgar kept his distance, and had been replaced by Mr. Redmond, on whose arm Alice seemed perpetually to hang; and by the evident delight on his face, he seemed happy to endure the weight.

Emma could not but wonder at what had happened between Alice and Edgar, and whether it offered her an opportunity. She recalled how well her reintroduction to Edgar had gone, that famous Sunday morning on the churchyard green; they might have talked all day and on into evening, had they not been interrupted. It seemed only when they were in the company of others that they grew awkward and uncertain. With Ralph now gone, and with Edgar divided from Alice, might she hope for a second chance with him? She considered how she might contrive a meeting.

But this ambition was derailed by a bulletin from Mrs. Curtis—and by a series of equally interesting revelations that followed, so that at the close of the afternoon Emma found herself with much to think on, and not all of it felicitous.

"I have just come from the Lodge," Mrs. Curtis said, bustling into Graftings and depositing her basket and cloak with the footman, "and what do you think! They have had a letter from Ralph. He has vowed on his life to return by the twenty-eighth." And here she hiked her skirt an inch from the floor and executed a few dainty steps in a giddy effusion. "The success of our dance is assured, now that the most dashing of our young swains will be there to enchant all the ladies."

Emma made note of that "*our* dance," but forbore to comment. "I am glad to hear of it," she said, in a tone which expressed the very opposite. Even Mrs. Curtis heard the glumness in it, and dropped her skirt, seizing instead her niece's arm in a fit of regret.

"I did not mean that the ladies would share *equally* in his attentions, my dear," she said with great urgency. "Only that he is so gallant, he will make sure none goes away unhappy. But I am certain there is only one whose happiness is the very fulcrum of his own."

Emma felt her face burn in irritation, and said, "Whoever she is, I am very glad for her." But Mrs. Curtis must have seen her color, for she smiled and squeezed her forearm and said, "As you very well should be, you dear, sly tease! Now I must hurry and tell your mother the news; what transports it will cause her!"

Despite her vexation, Emma nearly laughed; she had never known her mother to be transported. The imagination beggared at what might be sufficient to accomplish it, but it was certainly not the attendance at a dance of a rakish young gentleman less than half her age. Such a creature, however, might have been specifically invented to transport Mrs. Curtis.

As her aunt scurried off toward the drawing room, Emma begged her pause a moment and satisfy her on a single count. "Is Miss Nesmith to attend?" she asked.

"Why, Emma," was the reply; "what an unnatural creature you are! Have you not insisted on knowing from your mother everyone on the guest list?"

"I have not," said Emma, shocked at the idea that she would behave so intemperately.

Mrs. Curtis shook her head as though in despair of the girl; then looked up brightly and said, "Yes, but of course Miss Nesmith will be here. She is *my* particular friend, even if she is no longer yours."

A sharp retort formed on Emma's tongue; but she stilled it, as she still wanted intelligence. "I am glad of it. I have yet to see her with Mr. Redmond. I hear that they are quite sweethearts."

To her surprise, Mrs. Curtis's face fell into the most unbecoming scowl. "I can assure you, *that* is but the most fleeting of fancies," she said with uncharacteristic sharpness. "I begin to lose patience with Alice, the way she insists on pursuing what she does not want."

Emma was deeply confused. "So…she is no longer attached to him?"

"She is not. Although," Mrs. Curtis amended, somewhat reluctantly, "she may not quite know it yet. But she shall be *made* to know it. And she shall be reminded where her heart truly resides, and exhorted not to forget it."

With that, Mrs. Curtis wheeled about and departed the hall; and Emma, still reeling from the news—which was ominous to her in ways she was not yet able to understand —was on the point of doing the same, when the door flung open again and Frances came tumbling in, tugging on her spaniels' collars while the two creatures snarled savagely at something just outside.

"Dash! Cannon! I will not remind you a fourth time!" Frances exclaimed; and when she had yanked them into submission, she called out the door, "Perhaps it would be best if you left Magnate tethered to the post, Joseph." An unintelligible reply followed; after which Frances noticed Emma in the hall. "We have been out walking," she explained—referring, as ever, to herself and Mr. Denham.

"Whom she calls 'Joseph,'" Emma could not help observing privately.

Suddenly intrigued by the mystery of her sister's constant attendance by this older neighbor, Emma was moved to comment, "It seems you are seldom independent of each other, these days."

Anyone but Frances might have responded guardedly, if not taken offense; but Frances merely shrugged and said, "We are good friends; we have a strong affinity."

"It is a pity your dogs do not share it," thought Emma. But she strove to be less confrontational in her actual reply: "I would give much to have a friend whose company I found so enduringly agreeable."

Frances gave her a wary look, as if suspecting something satirical had been said at her expense; but at that moment Mr. Denham entered looking mildly disheveled, and said, "I think Magnate will be contented there for the moment—and in the meantime, I should very much like a court plaster." He displayed his hand, on which a bite mark had begun to well with blood.

"Oh, I did not see that happen!" Frances exclaimed, examining the wound. "Which of these naughties did that to you?"

"Cash," said Mr. Denham, before shaking his head and correcting himself: "Dannon." He was clearly very distraught.

"Robert," Frances said to the footman, "tell Mrs. Hicks that Mr. Denham requires a court plaster."

"And a brandy," said Mr. Denham.

"And a…never mind," she said, turning back to him with a stern look.

"Purely medicinal!" he said pleadingly—and then he too noticed Emma. "Good afternoon, Miss Emma."

"I have just been on the point," Frances said, "of telling Emma of our project."

He gave her a questioning look. "Are you certain?"

"I am. She has developed a curiosity about us," she said, throwing Emma a disapproving look, "and it's as well she knew the truth now, to save her sniffing after us like a bloodhound."

"There is very little danger of *that*," Emma said with some disgust.

"Be that as it may, here is what you wish to know: Mr. Denham and I are in the process of establishing an association dedicated to safeguarding the integrity of English dog breeding. It will be a society of like-minded owners and enthusiasts, and will formalize regulations and standards by which we may preserve the excellence of each breed and forestall degeneration of its line."

"Who determines these regulations and standards?"

"We do," said Frances, placing her hand briefly on Mr. Denham's arm. "At least, it is we who will present the first draft—which is what we have been so industriously composing. Other members may then suggest alterations or amendments."

The conversation might have gone further had Hicks not vaulted in with a court plaster of sufficient size to service a battlefield surgery, and drawn all the attention of the room to her nervous clicking and commotion as she trimmed it down to size—seeming, at least to Emma, almost disappointed that there was no more grievous a wound with which she might better distinguish herself. As she tended Mr. Denham, she and the footman gently led him away into an adjoining room, as though his injury required aid in walking. He protested against the fuss, but did suggest that a brandy would be of great benefit to him.

Emma did not know whether to be dazzled or disdainful of Frances's very peculiar plan; but she was left feeling somewhat envious that there was so much in her sister's life that accommodated her energy and intelligence. She was jealous that, however, bizarrely, Frances was *challenged*.

She was still fixed upon the spot in the hall where Mrs. Curtis had left her, and was once again on the point of departing it when another surprise forestalled her. For who should appear from the back of the house but Violet, the disgraced housemaid—whom Emma knew to be forbidden to venture upstairs.

"I beg your pardon, miss," she said, averting her eyes and executing a small curtsey—smaller than usual, for she was grown even more ungainly than Emma had last seen her. The child within her would soon make itself known.

"Let me beg *yours*," Emma said; "for I must ask, ought you to be here? I would not wish you to suffer another rebuke from Mrs. Hicks."

"Miss Frances called for me to come up," she said almost pleadingly. "It's the dog," she explained, pointing towards the front door; "I have a way with animals, I'm told, and Miss Frances asked for me to go and sit with Mr. Denham's Magnate, and keep him from fretting."

The past quarter-hour had been so very strange that Emma merely took this in stride. "Well, then, you had best attend to it."

Violet humbly made her way across the hall towards the door; and when she was directly before Emma, she unexpectedly looked up and locked eyes with her; and Emma had the astonishing sense that the girl was about to tell her something—and what's more, something vital.

But it was a fleeting moment; the girl lost her nerve, lowered her gaze, and hurried out the door.

CHAPTER FIFTEEN

Mr. Nesmith was coming to regret that the Marlows had returned to Graftings. This was not on account of any misconduct by the family itself—for the parson must admit they behaved exactly as they should. And Sir Godfrey and his lady had donated seven pounds towards the church organ, which was handsome indeed.

Rather it was their effect on others, which might be called deranging, that had Mr. Nesmith harkening back fondly to the days when they were in absentia. In particular his daughter Alice had become a creature wholly unknowable to him. She had, admittedly, been willful and defiant of him in the past; but he might comfort himself that at least he knew her mind. Now it defeated him to deduce any motive in what she was about.

She had for a time curbed her restlessness and permitted Edgar Willmot to pay court to her; and Mr. Nesmith allowed himself to nurse hopes in that direction, as young Willmot was nothing like his brother: a decent if colorless sort, and the son of his patron besides. But his attentions abruptly ceased and Alice offered no word of explanation for it; and Mr. Nesmith had learned better than to ask.

Yet instead of repining or exhibiting what the parson had considered the usual languishing behavior of females who have loved in vain, Alice had, within days, hurled herself almost bodily at the verger, Mr. Redmond; and while

Mr. Nesmith had often considered this a desirable match, he had been thinking that it was Redmond who would by degrees persuade his daughter to consider him; not in his wildest fancies had he imagined that Alice would be the one to pursue and claim him like a buck she had tracked, shot dead, and hauled home for skinning and salting.

But he had accustomed himself to the situation because in this case, at least, he thought the end might excuse the means. And yet now, with no reason apparent to Mr. Nesmith, Alice had tossed aside his verger like a pear that had been kept too long that had gone overripe. Redmond himself was clearly mystified by his sudden dismissal, and had fallen into a kind of bewilderment that prevented him from adequately performing his duties. Just the prior Sunday he had placed the church Bible on the lectern open to the page Mr. Nesmith had directed (Ephesians 6:10-24), but upside-down, so that Mr. Nesmith must either crane his neck absurdly to read it, or take up the weighty volume and strive to put it right; an undignified choice and in either case, certain to prompt laughter—as indeed it did, especially when Mr. Nesmith, who had chosen the second course of action, set the book down on his own thumb, and was distinctly heard to swallow a most un-Christian epithet. In revenge for the mirth at his expense, he fed the parishioners such a lengthy assurance of their ultimate damnation that he was confident none of them slept but ill for several days thereafter.

Alice, for her part, was so serene of countenance that she might never have heard of Mr. Redmond at all. The whole of her attention was turned to a dance being held at Graftings at the end of the month, for which she insisted she must have a new dress; she had none suitable for so fine an occasion. To which he had replied, then she would certainly do well to make one, and to lose no time at it, for he had heard such things required more than a day's endeavor. She had seethed for a bit—being no seamstress, as he knew (but only for her want of application)—and yet she outwitted him again by inviting Mrs. Curtis to help her in the gown's manufacture. Admitting Mrs. Curtis into the house was like allowing it to be overrun by budgerigars, and there were occasions when her chatter was so intrusive that the parson was driven to conduct his studies outside the house, beneath the shade of a maple tree.

Where, alas, he could still somewhat hear her.

What he feared was that Alice intended once again to set her cap at Ralph Willmot. He had thought Ralph safely in London—though perhaps "safely" was not the word, since it was rumored Ralph's time in town was chiefly spent brawling and getting shot at—but one of Mrs. Curtis's constant refrains was that he would be back in time for the dance—*on purpose* for the dance, in point of fact. It seemed possible to Mr. Nesmith that his daughter had grown bored by such steady, reliable figures as Edgar Willmot and Mr. Redmond, and begun craving the excitement and unpredictability provided by an unrepentant cad.

The prospect so alarmed him that he took greater notice of his daughter than was his usual habit; he meant to watch her for signs that her aim was anything but what it should be. He even briefly considered attending the dance himself—he had received an invitation—though an evening spent with his parishioners at what he considered their worst, heaped with frippery and immersed in light music and lighter conversation, was not to be borne for any reason; not even the rescue of his daughter's reputation.

No, he would dine as planned with Mr. Curtis—who also preferred to steer clear of such frolics—and they would take their meal over a game of chess, during which, if their history together was any indication, scarcely two dozen words would be spoken altogether. It would be a very agreeable evening.

Farther north, in town, another man despaired of a reputation—this one his own. Ralph Willmot had, due to more than usually intemperate behavior, found himself banned from yet another of his preferred public houses, reducing the number in which he might easily disport himself to no more than a handful; he had also, through expectation of soon marrying well, taken rather more risks at the gaming table than was strictly prudent, and as a result now found himself very suddenly and very seriously in debt.

Which made it all the more pressing that this project of wedding an heiress be seen to its completion. And while his time in town had been meant to soften the heart of his principal candidate, Miss Emma Marlow, to his suit, it had had rather the opposite effect; for he had been examining the possibility of alternative nominees for his bride and had come up alarmingly short. True, there were many very rich and very handsome young women who might creditably fit the bill; and he had been introduced to many of them by means of his friendship with their brothers.

But alas, those very same fellows were those who knew best the kind of man he was; and while they considered Ralph in many ways their champion for the heroic fearlessness with which he drank, danced, wooed, and wagered, these were very far from the qualities that might recommend him as a brother-in-law.

In short, his name was so blackened on the rolls of marriageable bachelors that the hope extended by Miss Emma Marlow grew ever dearer to him.

Edgar and Emma

To do him credit, this was not her only appeal to him. She was a very fine-looking girl, possessed of a delightful spirit. He was wise enough to know that that spirit might come to plague him; for a girl of Miss Emma Marlow's temper was unlikely to look kindly on deviations from the marriage vows, and would certainly find many ingenious ways to make him *feel* her displeasure; but he must bear that as best he can. He envied his father in this regard; for so oblivious to fault was Mrs. Willmot that all the excesses of Babylon might parade through her sewing room, and she would not look up from her tent-stitch.

Indeed, Miss *Frances* Marlow would be more likely to remain unconscious of lapses in spousal fidelity, and to forgive them if they did intrude on her notice; and by the strictest rules of propriety, as the eldest daughter she ought to be first to wed. And Ralph had tried her, long ago, when she was fourteen; but even then she was proof against his charm. He seemed barely able to retain her attention for the duration of a single sentence. He had even recruited his dog into the attempted courtship, and that had awakened her enthusiasm—but not, alas, for him. Though had Bravo at that moment gained the power of speech and declared himself, she would gladly have accepted him.

So it must be Emma. And even the propriety owed to birth order seemed to be no longer a consideration, as Ralph was fairly certain that Miss Frances Marlow would soon be Mrs. Joseph Denham. Never mind that this gentleman was more than twice her age; Ralph was not blind to the ties of genuine affection. In fact, he liked to flatter himself that he alone of all those who called Marlhurst home could see what was plainly in front of his nose.

Take his brother. Ralph knew for a certainty that Edgar pined for Emma—Edgar, who took no notice of any young lady. And he knew as well that Emma was not insensible to Edgar in return. But this, he was persuaded, was merely the lingering effect of a juvenile adventure they had shared, involving a snake, that had briefly made them romantic heroes in village lore. And that had been a very long time ago; Edgar had lost whatever dash he had then possessed, and Emma had grown more spirited and more passionate, and far less likely to find true companionship with a man whose deepest feelings were for events that occurred twenty-five hundred years before.

He did not glory in being more attractive than Edgar; nor would he account it a triumph to win Miss Emma Marlow away from him. For he loved his brother, and he pitied him; bookish men seldom found wives, and seldom made them happy when they did.

And yet there was a small thread of selfishness that wove through his fraternal affection; which is that Ralph enjoyed Edgar's rapt attention and enduring admiration. It was just as well that Edgar's life was lived principally in the pages of dust-caked books, because it made him all the more susceptible to Ralph's tales of his own adventures, whenever the two brothers met. Edgar, for Ralph, was the mirror in which he saw himself reflected; and any alteration in Edgar would mean a kind of death for Ralph.

But there was small enough worry of that. And he could reassure himself of it very soon, as he had received an invitation to a dance at Graftings on the twenty-eighth, along with a letter from his mother entreating him to attend, for she greatly missed his company. And as it would be advantageous for him to slip away from his creditors in town, and skulk back to Marlhurst until he had secured the means to satisfy them (that being Miss Emma Marlow's hand, and Miss Emma Marlow's fortune), had made ready to go.

Edgar and Emma

But he was not entirely without apprehension; for while he had taken care to conduct himself unimpeachably while in his home county, he had suffered an occasional lapse; one in particular, of a very embarrassing nature. It would be very unfortunate were this regrettable blunder to derail his current plan.

But as he had no alternative, it must be risked. And so: to Sussex!

CHAPTER SIXTEEN

"I believe we may congratulate ourselves, my dear," said Sir Godfrey to his lady some hour and more into the dance. "Everywhere I look I see enjoyment; and everywhere I am met with countenances beaming amity and gratitude. I cannot think what more we might have desired."

Emma overheard this burst of effusion from her father, and her mother's more sedate but equally contented reply; and to give them their due, the dance was in many ways unfolding exactly as planned. The assembled guests included many of whom the family had seen little since their return to Marlhurst, and there was an eagerness to rekindle long-neglected friendships. Emma was delighted to be reacquainted with a number of young ladies and gentlemen whom she would not have recognized, so altered had they become in the five-year interval since last she saw them— as, they insisted, had she. The orchestra—hired from town —was very fine, and inspired even the most taciturn of the revelers to hazard a few steps; and when they took a quarter-hour break to refresh themselves, Miss Diana Ashe, the neighborhood's most accomplished young lady in matters musical, consented to play the pianoforte so that the dancing might continue unimpeded.

But for all that, there were some troubling undercurrents —minor notes of discord that threatened, if unchecked, to turn the general harmony into a regrettable cacophony.

Most evident of these was Mrs. Curtis, who on arrival had heard from Lady Marlow—who had only received word of it herself that afternoon—that Tom Peake would not be in attendance. He was not yet, he had confessed, so confident in his ability to maneuver through the many obligations required of him by his masters that he felt comfortable abandoning them for even so short a time as the dance would have demanded.

"What poppycock," Mrs. Curtis said to Emma, with such force that were there a sibilant anywhere within the phrase, it could be said that Mr. Curtis spat. "The idea that the drudgeries of university life might not be leavened by occasional frivolity! Among a man's own kin, no less! Who are these masters, I ask you? Who are they to declare such a thing? Do they not know who Tom is? Do they not comprehend that he is the foster-son of a baronet?"

"I believe there are many at Cambridge who may boast much higher that that, Aunt," said Emma; "and they are held to the same standard."

But that was not all that rankled Mrs. Curtis; for not only had Tom disappointed her, but Ralph Willmot had yet to appear.

"If he does not come, without having sent word," said Mrs. Curtis in a high choler, "I shall have done with him; I swear I shall. If he does not come, he will not know my forgiveness—no, he shall not; not for anything less than a broken limb. *Two* broken limbs," she amended, "because with only one, he might yet have written."

Emma laughed in good-natured horror. "Aunt! You are too severe. It is but a dance. I trust there will be many others."

"*You* will forgive him, then," said Mrs. Curtis, softening; she patted Emma's arm. "And that is all that matters. That will be my solace and my comfort."

This so unnerved Emma that she strove to put it out of her mind; and this was easily done, for she was drawn into the dance by Mr. Simon Shaw, and was happily occupied for the next several minutes in a spirited quadrille. But in the course of moving about the floor, up the length of the room and then circling back again, she had occasion to pass the other dancers, both singly and in formation, and was thus confronted at intervals with two figures of very great interest to her: Edgar Willmot and Alice Nesmith, who seemed to be partners—to his evident consternation, and her unmistakable exultation.

This was a juxtaposition made even more unsettling by the sight of Mr. Redmond, the verger, looking on from the perimeter of the room with an aspect of the sheerest misery; and after the dance, when Emma sought him out and could not find him, she was told that he had complained of a chill and gone home.

Emma could only begin to piece together what any of this might signify; was Alice using Edgar to make Mr. Redmond jealous—or had she used Mr. Redmond to inflame Edgar's passion and was now enjoying her success? Alas, her conjecture was interrupted; but in a most welcome manner. It was Edgar himself who intruded on her introspection, and asked whether, if she were not too fatigued by the quadrille, she might join him in a waltz.

Emma accepted, even as she espied Alice surging up from behind, like a wave that would crash down around Edward and wash him back into her possession. Emma presented her hand to Edgar, who led her out to the floor while Alice glowered as fearfully as any gorgon.

Edgar and Emma

The thrilling sensation of having thwarted her nemesis —however briefly—lifted Emma's spirits; so that after a few spins around the floor, when Edgar appeared to her to be searching for something to say to her, she was only too happy to assume the burden herself.

"I am sorry that I have seen you so little, Mr. Willmot," she said with what she hoped was the right balance of lightness and sincerity; "for I have found myself wondering about the progress of your literary project. Did I tell you?— of course I did not; we have not spoken since—but I found a copy of Plutarch in my father's library, and I took it down and have been attempting it."

He gave her a look of sheer wonderment. "Have you really? And how do you find it?"

"Very interesting," she said. "It certainly satisfies one's craving for narrative; there is so much *incident* that it can be overwhelming. I find I cannot take very much at a single sitting."

"Ah, yes, that is so," said Edgar, who had been known to immerse himself in that very text from sunup to sundown.

"And I must confess that from time to time I have some difficulty with the idiom. From which I have concluded that the time has come indeed for a new English translation."

She had expected him to beam at her; but he looked instead very dejected. "I thank you for that validation," he said, "but I have had to set that endeavor aside for the moment."

"That is too bad!" she exclaimed. "And how long do you anticipate this moment shall last?"

He laughed, but not at all merrily. "Some several decades, I expect," he said. When she gave him a puzzled look, he explained: "I have bowed both to my father's will, and to my destiny as the inheritor of Willmot Lodge and all its attendant properties."

She pouted prettily. "And is Willmot Lodge so jealous of your time that it will not accommodate any competitors for it?"

"Perhaps not; but Plutarch is. And so the result must be the same."

They were, by Emma's estimation, halfway through the tune, and she had not yet spoken in earnest to him; she must be more direct. "And yet there was an element of your own to the project, I seem to recall," she said now; "some innovation, was there not? You were about to tell me of it that morning on the church green, before we were interrupted."

He seemed charmed that she would recall this, and readily explained his plan to append a biography of a British luminary to each set of Greek and Roman lives. "So that to Plutarch's texts on Alexander, the greatest Greek general, and Julius Caesar, the greatest Roman, I will add my own life of Oliver Cromwell." He looked at her expectantly.

She began by gratifying him—"What a scheme; both audacious and worthy!"—but she could not resist, now that he had taken her into his confidence, becoming playful with him. "And yet, Cromwell, you say?—That is your choice for the greatest British general? Not Marlborough?"

He pleased her by going quite red in the face. "An argument may certainly be made for Marlborough. But I feel Cromwell was more analogous to Alexander and Caesar. Like them, he re-made the state. And like them, his innovations did not long survive him."

Edgar and Emma

"And yet Alexander and Caesar were exalted for long after—for *ever* after, given that we still revere them today. Whereas Cromwell has been despised and vilified."

He displayed a nervous smile. "I believe I have explained, have I not, that the purpose of the *Lives* is to compare the subjects' similarities *and* differences."

"And yet," she said, "Marlborough is closer to our own age and temperament; and closer to your own class." Here she knew she was being ingenuous; the Willmots, however ancient their name, were no more than landed gentry. But she desired to flatter him. "I think you have not given him due consideration," she said with a feline smile. "In fact, Mr. Willmot—if you will forgive me for being so bold—I think sometimes you are too swift to make a choice; you will allow pressure or persuasion to steer you from what might truly benefit you, to what might be considered most convenient."

He gave her a look as though, despite leading her in the dance, he was striving to follow her. "I am not entirely certain I take your meaning," he said. "You are saying—you are saying that I—"

"That you will settle for Cromwell when you might have Marlborough," she said, and by an exquisite fluke of timing the phrase was uttered just as Edgar turned Emma on the floor so that she was exactly adjacent to Alice (who had found a partner of her own); for a single heartbeat, the two girls might be seen side-by-side.

He could not but take her meaning; she was certain of it.

The tune concluded; the couples applauded the players, bowed, and separated. Edgar thanked her for honoring him, and asked whether she might do so again, perhaps for the rigadon. She said it would give her the greatest pleasure.

With that, Emma—somewhat flushed from the dancing —made her way to the punch bowl to take a bit of refreshment; meanwhile, couples lined up for the next number. But before the orchestra could begin there was an interruption; someone had taken the center of the room and was asking for the guests' attention.

Emma turned, and was astonished to see that it was Mr. Denham.

"I thank you for your kind indulgence," he said, "and will not exasperate you by laying claim to it for more than a moment. But I have chosen—that is, *we* have chosen this moment," he said, and here he extended his arm—and Emma might have been turned upside-down and back again with no less sensation than she felt at seeing Frances join him and take his hand—"to share with our friends the news that Miss Marlow has done me the great courtesy of consenting to be my wife."

This was followed by a spontaneous burst of applause; but Emma felt only the need to rejoin her mother and father, whom she strongly suspected had known no more of this arrangement than she herself, or they would surely have spoken of it.

They greeted her with looks of such blank shock that it was clear they were yet reeling from the unexpectedness of the announcement. Emma had but a moment to ascertain that in spite of this veritable ambush they were quite well and in aid of nothing, and then Frances and Mr. Denham were upon them, buffeting them with smiles, and they must all shake off their stupefaction and conduct themselves with as much dignity as could be managed.

"That was swift work, Denham," said Sir Godfrey as he shook his future son-in-law's hand. "We have not been back at Graftings but a month and a quarter." He withdrew his hand and scowled. "I had thought it the custom for a gentleman to acquire the father's blessing prior to an undertaking such as this."

Mr. Denham could manage no more than a sickly, nervous smile; but Frances said, "Papa, how old fashioned you are! And what a ridiculous scene that would have made, with Denham so much older than you! And anyway, if you had said no, I should have eloped. So, la!"

This so thoroughly disconcerted Sir Godfrey that he could do no more than sit down.

Mr. Denham, whose forehead had by this time filmed with sweat, said, "It may seem 'swift work,' as you say, Sir Godfrey, but I assure you, the affinity I share with your daughter is of very long standing."

"Of course it is," said Frances, placing her hand on her fiancé's arm. "Papa, do you not recall, it is through Mr. Denham that we acquired Dash and Cannon! He was with us on the very day."

"So I was," said Denham; "and with my great bitch, Fury."

"Magnificent beast" exclaimed Frances. "The noblest that ever lived. How you must feel her loss, even today!"

To everyone's wonderment, Mr. Denham's eyes brimmed with tears, and he turned abruptly away to conceal his great emotion.

For a moment all were at a loss for words; but Lady Marlow soon came to the rescue. "And how was this happy understanding reached?" she asked with as much grace as she could muster.

Frances beamed her delight at being able to tell the story. "We were at work on the particulars of our proposed society," she said, "when all at once my dear Mr. Denham wondered which of us ought to own it; and I said he must, because he has the connections to establish it and the means to fund it. But he said I must, because I have the youthful zeal to run it. And I said what a pity we were not one person; and he blushed up to his eyebrows, the dear thing, and said, 'What then if we were one person in the eyes of God?' And I asked whether that was a proposal of marriage, and he said that it was, and I accepted and then we got back to work."

"And when is the wedding to be?" asked Emma.

"We will marry at Christmas, at Mr. Denham's house."

"What?" cried Sir Godfrey. "At Waylands—here in Sussex? But we spend Christmas in Wiltshire!"

"I am sorry, Papa; but with all there is to do, I cannot be wed earlier, and would not be wed later."

"But would you not be wed elsewhere?"

She sadly shook her head. "Waylands boasts extensive kennels, so that Mr. Denham's friends from other counties may bring their dogs."

"That is the most singular thing I have ever heard," said Sir Godfrey, his face now showing signs of the struggle to suppress his feeling. "Dogs, at a wedding?"

"Indeed!" enthused Frances. "I am more eager to see them than to meet their masters!"

Sir Godfrey continued to bluster. "And where will you reside until then? You cannot think to remain at Graftings on your own."

"I will stay with my Aunt Curtis until the wedding," said Frances casually.

"And has my sister agreed to this plan?"

Frances shrugged. "I have not yet proposed it; but I think she cannot refuse me."

"Perhaps not; but your Uncle Curtis can refuse to board your dogs."

"Oh, Dash and Cannon may stay at Graftings, and I shall visit them every day. Surely there can be no impropriety in *that*."

She was drawn away by another offer of congratulation; and when her back was turned, Lady Marlow patted her husband's hand and said, "Never mind, my dear; she lived with us for seven months in Chipping Norton, where it was very inconvenient for her and her pets, and did so without complaint; so I think we must allow her these liberties now."

Emma could remember quite a bit of complaint; though wisely, none of it directed at her father and mother. But she said nothing; she had resolved to be happy for her sister.

But Sir Godfrey was not so easily appeased. "She has made these plans on her own, let her realize them on her own," he said angrily. "We shall Christmas as always at Dunfosters, and send her our compliments on the wedding day."

In such turbulent waters as these, it seemed a genuine relief when at length a rigadon was called; and Emma, eager to honor her commitment to Edgar, went in search of him —but was intercepted by Mrs. Curtis, who bubbled more vivaciously than the champagne.

"Oh, my dear Emma, you will never guess who has just come in!"

But of course Emma guessed immediately; no one—not Lord Nelson, not the Prince Regent, not the Empress of Russia—could have prompted her aunt to such ecstasies.

"I think it must be Mr. Ralph Willmot," she said drily.

"But how foolish of me, of *course* you guessed!" Mrs. Curtis exclaimed. "For surely he is foremost in your mind to a degree even exceeding my own!" She looked over her shoulder. "Where has he got to? I swear to you, he was directly to the back of me but a moment ago." At which a small knot of revelers parted briefly, and Ralph stepped forth from their midst. "Here, Mr. Willmot!" Mrs. Curtis cried, too shrilly, and she waved both her arms as though attempting to summon him via semaphore. "Here we are—and I have found her for you, just as I promised! My dear niece, Miss Emma Marlow! Come and see!"

Emma did not like the sound of that; for why should Ralph have sent her aunt in search of her? But it was too late to evade him; he was before her, bowing over her hand.

"And now my joy must be considered complete," Mrs. Curtis breathlessly declared, "and all my earthly labors as well; I may with all contentment meet my maker this very night. For now," she said, retreating somewhat awkwardly from hyperbole, "I am to be rewarded with the sight of this handsome couple dancing!"

"Perhaps in due time," Emma said, "but this dance I am promised to another."

Ralph shook his head. "Ah, but Miss Emma, I believe you are forgetting something: you owe me a debt."

She furrowed her brow. "I beg your pardon, sir? A debt, you say?"

"Yes," he said, leaning in so that Mrs. Curtis might not hear. "Before I left for town, we wagered on your sister's engagement to Mr. Denham; and I have won. I told you then, I would decide the manner of repayment after my victory; and so I have. I demand this dance."

Emma felt herself growing flustered. "But—but I have promised it to your brother!"

Ralph's features relaxed, as though this were no difficulty at all. "Oh, Edgar will not mind it; I assure you."

"I think any man must mind being denied something that was previously promised to him," she protested.

150

Edgar and Emma

"As for example," he said cunningly, "a man who was promised the payment of a debt in whatever coin he chose? Eh? Miss Emma Marlow? Is it of *that* that you speak?"

It was hopeless; he had boxed her in. No—she had done that herself, weeks before, when she had so carelessly allowed him to entrap her.

Edgar now came up between them. "Hello, Ralph," he said; "I am glad you are here." He turned to Emma. "The rigadon begins, Miss Emma; if we do not hurry, we will miss it entirely."

Ralph chose this moment to take Emma's hand and make as if to draw her away; it was an unnecessarily cruel gesture, and she disdained him for it. "I am sorry," she said with as much sincerity as she could pour into the phrase; "I cannot now explain, but your brother has exercised a right that is of longer standing than my pledge to you. I know it is unforgivable, but I hope you will forgive it all the same."

And then she was out of earshot; and for the next several minutes Ralph led her about the floor, praising her generosity, extolling her beauty, and regaling her with amusing stories of his misadventures in London; but she only affected to listen, hearing no more than one word in ten. She was desperate for the end of the dance, that she might find Edgar and make amends to him for this awful humiliation.

As for Edgar himself, he too found himself on the receiving end of an endless stream of verbiage, as Mrs. Curtis exhausted every superlative she knew in her attempt to do justice to the picture Ralph and Emma made together; and like Emma he barely took in a word of it.

He had hoped to speak further with Emma on the matter of choice, with which she had so slyly teased him, for he had not quite apprehended her meaning; though he had a rough idea—more a hope than a notion, if he were honest—that she had used Cromwell and Marlborough as a metaphor for Alice and herself; by which means she must be encouraging him to dare a declaration to her.

But that was all foolishness, as became blindingly apparent the moment Ralph appeared and demonstrated that Emma was his abject slave. All rules were to be broken for Ralph; and in truth he did not begrudge his brother—for Ralph was everything Edgar was not, and that must account for something. He wished it did not account for Emma being lost to him; but he was a humble man, and had learned to accept his limitations.

Except…that Emma had encouraged him *not* to do that very thing. And he still could not make sense of why, could not discern what she expected of him, and what choice he had made that she found so regrettable.

He replayed their conversation, from start to finish, in his mind; and then it became clear.

In fact, the more he considered it, the wiser and more sagacious did Emma seem in having perceived his failing, and to have offered him a framework in which he might see it himself.

Wonderful girl!—he owed her his freedom.

He espied Alice in the middle distance; she was headed his way.

Well, he need endure none of *that* any longer. Emma had opened his eyes. His life would comprise many difficulties, he was certain; but none of them here, and none of them now.

He begged Mrs. Curtis's pardon—she was so startled by his interruption, it seemed likely that she had forgotten she was in company with anyone at all—and went to the end of the room, then out the French doors and onto the terrace, where he hoped to clarify his newfound resolve with the benefit of a moment's fresh air and solitude.

But the latter was to be denied him; for he found his sister Patience had already claimed it.

"I beg your pardon," he said; and he was about to retreat when he noted something different about her aspect —something that gave him pause.

She was looking very well; much handsomer and more elegant than he had seen her in many years. He had not noticed it in, in the characteristic rush from the Lodge into the waiting carriage; but here, without the competition of other persons and their tumult, she could be seen to best advantage—and advantage it surely was.

But the effect was somewhat undercut by a wanness; almost a look of exhaustion. He asked, "Are you well?"

She considered this for a moment; then said, "I am not ill."

He suspected this to be an evasion, and so asked, "But perhaps...ailing?"

She turned away from him with rather too much abruptness. She was hiding her features from him.

He did not understand this. Patience had long been content to be a person of no consequence; she throve on humility and service. But something had clearly caused a ripple in her previously placid demeanor.

"Come," he said; "I would not have you gloomy! Will not your spirits lift at the sight of the young couples dancing?"

She turned and looked at him again; and the desolation on her face told him that the question had been ill chosen.

"I am sorry," she said. "I had expected to be merrier; that is all."

"And is there nothing that can be done to make you so?"

She lowered her head.

He sighed. "Then I will take you from this place. Come, sister; take my hand. We will have no languishing."

She looked at him with reluctant gratitude. "Oh, Edgar; no. I would not be the cause of your enjoyment being curtailed."

"My enjoyment is already so thoroughly curtailed, that the thought of home is most welcome to me." He waggled his fingers at her, to induce her to rise and take his hand.

"But," she protested, "should Mama require me…"

"Mama has company aplenty." In fact he had only just seen his mother at the card table, furiously immersed in a game of faro.

And so they departed, brother and sister, and shared a carriage ride home in a silence that was very agreeable to both. For Edgar in particular, it gave him a space of time to compose his thoughts and strategize the encounter he must now hazard.

The next afternoon a letter for Emma arrived at Graftings; she had been hoping to hear from Edgar, as his disappearance from the dance had greatly worried her—hence, with what relief did she open the missive.

And with what swiftness did that relief dissipate!

Dear Miss Emma,

Allow me to thank you for the inestimable benefit of your friendship—as I hope we may be considered friends—which last night brought me not only the transitory delight of a dance (though the grace of your step will long adorn my memory), but your wise counsel as well—couched so humbly and with such respect for my pride, that it nearly defeated me to comprehend your meaning; but at last I came to see your motive, and have this morning said good-bye to my Cromwell, and set a course for my Marlborough.

I hope someday to repay the service you have done me; in the meantime, I remain most abjectly in your debt.

Your servant
EDGAR WILLMOT

Emma puzzled over the letter, not knowing what sense to make of it; until at last Mrs. Curtis came to call later in the day, carrying great news—news which thrust Frances's engagement into a shadow:

Edgar Willmot had had it out with his father and had quitted the Lodge, intent on making his career as a fellow at Oxford; and thereto he had gone—"and when we will see him next, I cannot say," said Mrs. Curtis, who was clearly finding interest in Edgar for the first time in her life; "but I daresay when we do, he will be a don. Is that like a doctor, do you think? Will he cease to be Mr. Willmot and be instead Don Edgar?—I wonder who can tell me. Possibly my husband; but when I asked him this morning, he did not hear me."

Nor, now, did Emma, who on hearing the news unceremoniously fled up the stairs to her room. So great was her misery that it never occurred to her to announce that she was shutting herself up for the remainder of her life; despite which she remained there for three-and-a-half days—longer by far than she had ever done after declaring lifetime self-exile—and emerged hollow-eyed and pale, with her hair out of place, so that when she saw her, Jenny the lady's maid gave a start and dropped a pitcher of water, for which she had her ears boxed by Mrs. Hicks.

Book Two

CHAPTER SEVENTEEN

Edgar had delayed his return to Sussex long enough. It was the nineteenth of December, and the wedding of Mr. Denham and Miss Marlow was to be in three days' time. It was certainly not vital that he should be there; but nor was there a compelling reason to stay away. And while he dithered over a decision, the halls and grounds of Oxford had emptied around him, till it was possible to pass a quarter-hour traversing his lodgings to Professor Bridge's rooms without seeing a living soul.

The Professor himself was soon to depart, although it was not his habit to vacate at the Christmas holiday. His sole reason for making an exception this year was that he had had a letter from his sister, who had reliably promised him that this would be their aged mother's final yuletide.

"It is a gambit she attempts each December, without fail," the professor said as he poured out a glass of brandy-wine for Edgar, and another for himself. "It has come to be so much a part of the season for me that without it I should feel that I had missed some essential element—almost as if

I were not to hear 'O Magnum Mysterium' sung. And yet," he continued, as he handed the glass to Edgar, "this time I think she writes with more conviction than cajolery. She has not, for example—cheers, my dear—she has not attempted to persuade me with a list of alarming symptoms, many of which cannot but remind one of contemporary accounts of the Black Death. The absence of these alone is eloquent; for I have always thought they were meant to persuade she that wrote them as much as he to whom they were addressed. By which I can but conclude that Sophia is sincere in her belief that this is Mamma's valedictory nativity." He tossed back his sherry, then set down the glass on a small table—next to which his robes hung, looking resplendent in the candlelight. "I am considering taking my official vestments, which my mother has never seen, and in that way will perhaps both gratify her and overawe her into a more timely departure; so that my days with Sophia and her rather disagreeable husband and children may be curtailed. But I suspect I shock you."

"You do not," said Edgar, sipping at his own brandy. He had too often heard the professor speak disparagingly of his relations. Indeed it seemed that many of Edgar's mentors at Oxford were defiantly single men of late middle age; and while in his younger years he had seen something heroic in this, now he could not but feel a kind of pity for it. These rooms, for instance—so commodious, and yet so Spartan; as though Professor Bridge had earned by his academic achievements more space than his private life could fill. And yet there somehow managed to accrue pockets of clutter. A wife would have put all that right, Edgar knew; but the idea of a Mrs. Bridge was not one that Edgar had ever quite successfully conjured. Despite his towering height and large frame, the professor seemed to have accommodated for the lack of a spouse by incorporating those distaff attributes he felt most requisite into his own person; he fluttered across a room quite dantily, had a light and silvery laugh, and when the mood struck him could be openly flirtatious.

It was this last quality that had begun to concern Edgar; for he had now been at Oxford, in rented quarters, for several months and had not yet managed to obtain a teaching position at his old college. Professor Bridge, who encouraged him to keep at his translation of Plutarch in the meantime, seemed almost jealous over him, and saw to it that he kept largely to himself, while at the same keeping his hope alive, feeding him promising new developments just when Edgar was at his most despairing.

He did so now, turning away from his robes and affixing a look on Edgar's glass that seemed to say, "Still working on that, are we?" Then he grinned and said, "As for your own homeward journey, I think I may safely assure you that it may be undertaken in the knowledge that there will be progress of a kind to be celebrated when you return."

Edgar raised his eyebrows. "Indeed?"

The professor apparently decided not to wait for Edgar to finish his brandy, but to refill his own glass at once. "Professor Trotter has at long last succumbed to my entreaties, and has agreed to join me in recommending you for a fellowship," he said as he poured. "As since two existing fellows are all that is required for such a nomination, there you are."

This was more a substantial report that the professor's usual offering, so Edgar was inclined to optimism. "And the portfolio of my works? When may I submit it for examination? I have in mind a few alterations..."

"I have already submitted the latest manuscript of your Plutarch, which will serve admirably as a thesis," said the professor. The first sip of his second glass seemed to have cheered him. "It is a very fine piece of work, to date. And you are not unknown here and are well enough liked. So I think you may have every expectation of good news."

Thus Edgar was in fine spirits when he took his leave of the professor, and wished him the happiest of Christmases. As he headed back to his rooms—once again alone, but comforted by the presence of snow flurries, who struck him as being akin to guardian angels—he surprised himself by thinking of Emma. If his scholarly ambitions, so long stalled, were now to be realized, he could not but wonder whether he had been too precipitous in abandoning his hopes in that other direction.

It had, after all, been nearly a quarter of a year since he had left Emma literally in Ralph's arms, and in all that time there had been no announcement of an engagement. His mother, indeed, had recently voiced a kind of impatience on the matter, as though at a loss to understand what might be the delay.

The delay, Edgar hoped, might be that Emma and Ralph were proving to be less suited to each other than was supposed by everyone who wished them joy. Edgar knew Ralph's roving eye, and was appreciative of the length of time he had kept it firmly set on Emma; but he also knew that Ralph hated to lose, and could not but wonder whether his continued efforts to turn Emma's reluctance into acceptance were prompted by his own genuine feeling, or simply by his pride.

With what amounted almost to a promise of a fellow-ship when he returned, Edgar now felt a gambler's exhilaration and a longing to throw the dice again. And so when at last he reached his rooms, it was with a sudden energy to pack his things, that he might be able to depart the next morning—and with any luck be at Willmot Lodge by end of day.

It was on the very same morning that Edgar set out, that Emma awakened feeling unusually light-hearted.

She would not like to admit it, but the approach of Frances's nuptials had had its effect on her; for so flushed with happiness and expectation was her sister, that Emma thought her prettier than she had ever been before. She sparkled in company, where she was inevitably the focus of all attention; something Emma did not quite envy, and yet felt jealous of all the same. It was a paradox.

Even Mr. Denham—fleshy, pepper-haired, hobbling Mr. Denham—seemed transformed by the air of felicitation and congratulation into, if not quite a romantic hero, at least a younger and more vigorous gentleman than he had previously come near to giving any impression of being. His ability to bring a delighted smile to France's face merely by walking into a room could not be witnessed without feeling some residual bliss of one's own.

In short, an idea had formed in Emma's head that the wedded estate amended many of the difficulties that might have been present on going into it. Frances and Mr. Denham had seemed a comically unsuited pair when the notion of them as lovers had first been presented to her; but now she found it difficult to think of them separately. Affection, community, tradition—all the various components of wedlock as both a blessing and an institution—had come together to create a sum more than the equal of its parts.

Even her parents had come around. Sir Godfrey had got over the manner in which the couple had stolen a march on him; and they had agreed—as Frances must have known they would—to remain in Sussex for Christmas, so that Frances could be married from Graftings instead of Waylands. Sir Godfrey had even approved an emergency expansion of the kennels to accommodate the needs of Mr. Denham's dog-owning guests.

Emma was impressed; and she was inspired this morning—with the sunlight streaming through her windows as though equally confident of every happiness in her future—to apply the lesson to her own life.

Ralph Willmot had been an admirably steady suitor to her; she had not liked to admit it, but now she must. He had endured every rebuff and yet returned to her without any symptom of wounded vanity or aggrieved pride. He took every opportunity to flatter her, to charm her, to make her laugh—the stories of his haplessness in the role his father had now thrust on him (gentleman farmer and rural landlord of Willmot! was any role less suited for such as he?) had been known to reduce her to merry tears.

Twice he had asked her to marry him; twice she had said no. After the second time she had not seen him for a week; and though she had felt relief at that—perhaps she had got rid of him at last—was there not also a slight twinge of regret?—Almost of panic?

Because without Ralph, whither Emma? For she had resolved not to pine for Edgar; she must put aside, at long last, her girlish fantasy about her woodland rescuer. Even Alice Nesmith had grudgingly accepted her defeat in Edgar's departure from Sussex, and had with as much grace and good humor as possible gone back to the long-suffering verger.

But Emma had no other suitor. And for the daughter of a baronet, such was the thinness of the society hereabouts that she had begun to realize that Mr. Denham himself must be considered a veritable catch.

Ralph was a compendium of many attractive qualities and many very bad ones; but despite the latter—and this was crucial—she liked him. Was that enough, then, to build on? Would the mere acceptance of him begin to transform what had once been the pejorative into the superlative?

It was a fine winter's day, bright and cheerful, and she was tired of existing at the perimeter of Frances's life; she must reclaim her own and begin to live it again. She must take a risk. She must *dare*.

And so when Ralph came to call that afternoon, he found her at her most radiantly welcoming.

"If you have a particular question for me today, Mr. Willmot," she said, "I think you will find yourself better pleased with the answer."

CHAPTER EIGHTEEN

There were many compliments and much congratulation when Emma and Ralph shared their news; and Emma was pleased by the happiness she had brought to her parents with this announcement. Even Frances wished her joy; though she added confidentially, when Ralph could not hear, "How brave you are to take him on!"—which Emma thought a rather ungracious thing to say.

She felt for the first time like a grown woman, who had behaved responsibly and made a decision from the head and not the heart. She was proud of herself.

She had even asked Ralph that he keep the engagement secret, known only to the two families, until after Frances's wedding. She had no desire to draw attention from her sister. But of course she knew Ralph, and was fairly certain he was congenitally incapable of keeping anything secret; and she found she did not mind having the news leak out to stupefy the residents of Marlhurst. In particular she wished for Alice Nesmith to hear it as soon as possible; for it pleased her that Alice should know that she too had recovered from the loss of Edgar—that heartbreak had no more thwarted her passage through life than it had Alice's own.

As it happened, the granting of Emma's wish was already in hand; for Lady Marlow had a brief note delivered to Mrs.

Edgar and Emma

Curtis, informing her of the engagement and prevailing upon her to keep it in the strictest confidence. Mrs. Curtis immediately lit out to inform everyone in town, instructing each of them in turn that she must mention it to no one else on pain of Mrs. Curtis's sternest disapprobation.

Alice was very surprised by the news, and not at all discommoded by it; quite the contrary. It gave her new hope, where she had thought all hope dead forever.

She had only ever given up Edgar because of two seemingly insurmountable barriers to obtaining him: his career at Oxford, and his evident feeling for Emma. But now Emma had removed one of those obstacles; and the one that remained seemed suddenly much less daunting. Certainly of the two, it was the one Alice had a fairer bet of overcoming.

She must simply jettison Mr. Redmond once more— easily done; he was like a jacket, as easily doffed as donned —and then she would be free to pursue Edgar whenever she next saw him.

Which might be very soon indeed. True, he had not parted well with his father; there had been much talk in the village of the disgust with which Mr. Willmot condemned his eldest son's abandonment of his ancestral duties in favor of what the paterfamilias considered foppery and self-indulgence; and at least one Marlhurst lady had attested to hearing Mr. Willmot say that his son was "welcome no longer at the Lodge."

But that had been some months past, and Alice knew the cooling power of time and distance. It would surprise her very much if Edgar did not return for Christmas.

All at once, the prospects for the season ahead seemed much brighter to her.

For Mrs. Curtis herself, the news was equally welcome. Emma's engagement to Ralph had been her design from the beginning, as she told her husband over dinner that night; the idea had in fact come to her the very day she heard that the Marlows were to come back to Graftings.

"I am sure I never thought it would take me so long to manage it," she said as she happily spread a layer of butter onto a slice of fresh-baked rye bread, "but I am sure the young people of today are much more willful than they were when I was a girl; they must be *made* to see what is in their own best interests. Why, I wonder, must they resist to the end?"

"Because," said her husband very drily, "there would be little point in resisting *past* the end. I pray you, my dear, pass me the fricassee."

"Mr. Curtis, you are too satirical," she replied as she gratified his request. "You know precisely what I mean—which is, why is it that the young will cling to their stubbornness until it is no longer possible to do so? I call it pride; pride and folly…and perhaps more of the latter than the former."

"I bow to your expertise in the matter," said Mr. Curtis a bit acidly, as he helped himself from the platter.

But Mrs. Curtis had grown reflective. "Ralph Willmot and Emma I may now leave to their own devices, which I am certain are sufficient to see them through their wedding day. But I must do more for Alice; she has always been my second project, and no less dear to me for that. She is meant for Tom Peake, you see; and he is to return to Graftings for Christmas. I will fix it then, you may be sure. Oh, I know what you will say: she has already an understanding with the verger."

Mr. Curtis, who had turned his attention entirely to his meal, seemed very unlikely to have intended to say any such thing.

"But that I am sure is a great exaggeration," his wife continued. "Alice is a pretty and accomplished young girl who has every right to admiration; and in her present circumstances, Mr. Redmond is the only man at hand to gratify her. And I am certain he is a pleasant enough and adequately respectable fellow; though I have not heard your opinion of him, which might be more to his credit."

After a few moments, when it became clear that she would not hear Mr. Curtis's opinion of the verger anytime soon, she went on.

"But he is the kind of man—I wonder, Mr. Curtis, whether you agree—whose features I cannot recall thirty seconds after he leaves a room. At this very moment I am unable to conjure his face. Or his voice. One finds he… what is the word I seek?…he *evaporates*. Does he not, my dear? And Alice certainly deserves better than that.

"Now, Tom Peake!" she continued, nibbling idly at her bread. "He is from a fine family, and is a great, scholarly mind who already possesses the sagacity and bearing of a man twice his age. He wants only a little merriment to complete him…a little color. And Alice, who wants a degree of grandeur to complete hers, can supply it, as he can for her. Oh, it is the very thing! And it is within my grasp. You will not dissuade me, Mr. Curtis; you will not deter me."

Indeed, it was plentifully evident from his manner that he would do neither.

Ralph had dined with the Marlows and now returned on foot to Willmot Lodge, preferring to walk that he might enjoy a more leisurely pace at which to sip whisky from the hip flask he had successfully concealed during his visit at Graftings.

Such success was not due to any expert method on his part; he had merely tucked the flask into the interior pocket of his coat. Its outline might be plainly seen by anyone who bothered to look. But Ralph knew that people saw what they wished to see; it was the most agreeable thing about them, and the one most responsible for his own good fortune. He need only project the image of the man he desired to be taken for, and society would do the rest.

Indeed, he had finally persuaded his father to see him as ill-suited to the role of master of Willmot Lodge. He would not have minded the title, nor its income; but those were still Edgar's, alas, and would remain so, barring some legal action, which his father (scorning lawyers) seemed disinclined to take. But to have the duties *without* the title and income was out of the question. So he had, by emphasizing his enduring ignorance and incompetence in all things agricultural, brought Mr. Willmot at last to despair of him, and to turn instead to David, who though yet very young seemed to have been born for precisely this function.

And yet Ralph's escape was not complete; indeed, he found himself even more diabolically bound than before. For Mr. Willmot had now appointed Ralph to oversee his interests in a new business venture he had bought into, which was a sugar plantation on the Caribbean island of St. Lucia. Even worse, the assignment was open-ended, so that Ralph could not even comfort himself with the thought that it would be *only* for six months, or *only* for a year… what if he were to remain there five? Or seven?…Such a span of time in so remote a locale would surely derange him. He would end by putting a pistol to his head.

Edgar and Emma

So it was nigh on miraculous that Emma Marlow had chosen this moment finally to accept him. Though on reflection, he might have anticipated it; he had heard of the way in which one wedding magically suggests another, especially among ladies. But now, in addition to having his wife-to-be's fortune to settle his debts, he had a means of delaying—perhaps indefinitely—his departure for St. Lucia. First there must be a wedding—some months in the future, certainly; then he must be further excused, that he might do his duty by his house and sire an heir. Which of course meant a male heir. So should Emma be brought to bed of a girl, he must try again—and continue trying until the desired result was achieved. With any luck, the St. Lucia sojourn might be put off until his father died—at which point, nothing could compel him to go.

He could not but think warmly of Emma for this bounty of hope she had afforded him; and indeed he thought warmly of her in any case. Hemmed in as he was by debt and reputation, he was lucky that the only girl of means whose society was still open to him was also a girl whose many fine qualities he had come to hold dear. It was not a great passion that he felt for Emma; but it was very much a tender, companionable affection. He would strive to do right by her; he would repay the beneficence she had brought into his life by doing his utmost to make her happy.

The flask was now empty, and the lights of Willmot Lodge were bright in the middle distance. There was, he saw, a coach parked on the drive, and a trunk was being removed from its boot.

For it was at this very moment that Edgar had arrived home.

CHAPTER NINETEEN

Patience was the first to greet him, in the hall just inside the front door.

She embraced him warmly, then stood back with a smile. "The children have all gone to bed," she said; "it is only Mama and Papa and me sitting up. We heard the coach on the drive; I came out to see. Oh, Edgar, I had so hoped you would be home for Christmas!"

"I have missed the Lodge," he said, looking around the place as he doffed his coat; a valet quietly took it from him and disappeared. "You say it is only Mama and Papa sitting up? Is Ralph not with you?"

"We expect him at any moment," she said, taking him by the arm. "He has been at all day at Graftings."

"Graftings?" Edgar said, and he looked at her with sudden wariness.

"Yes," she said, and he could see behind her eyes that she was struggling to be kind. "There is great news from that quarter; we only heard it ourselves a few hours past, and have yet to congratulate Ralph ourselves."

Edgar let his eyes fall shut. "So she has accepted him at last."

"She has." Patience tried to tug him into motion, to bring him to their mother and father; but he stood his ground so firmly that she must give up the attempt. "I am sorry, Edgar; I think you held Miss Emma Marlow in some esteem yourself."

"I still do," he said. "Ralph's proprietorship cannot alter such a thing."

"No," she said, and an unreadable look crossed her face; "where there is true regard, many dissuasions will not suffice to dampen it." She cast her glance downward. "If only it were otherwise."

In a flash, Edgar realized that Patience had been disappointed; he had never suspected such a thing, and it gave him a rush of fellow feeling for her. He assumed, however, that her heartbreak was of a much older vintage than his— that it was something she had nursed these many years— and so preserved the privilege of putting his own, fresh hurt forward.

"How am I to congratulate him?" Edgar asked, his voice brittle with bitterness.

But this was no sooner asked than answered; for Ralph came in, all smiles, his face flushed by the stiffness of the winter wind and—Edgar could smell it—by the effects of equally stiff drink.

And Edgar's heart melted. Of course he must congratulate Ralph; no matter that his brother pursued his pleasure with such recklessness—he was prodigal with the results. When Ralph was happy, all were happy. And seeing evidence of his joy now, Ralph must feel it to.

"So our great pagan has returned to scowl and frown at our Christian revels," Ralph said, energetically shaking his hand. "I am very glad of it; it is the only yuletide tradition I cherish."

"I scowl at no Christian revels," Edgar said. "I merely set them in their historical context."

"You bring Apollo into the manger, and I applaud you for it," Ralph said; "for it excuses my bringing in Dionysos."

He made to extract his hand, but Edgar held it fast. "I think I must commend you on your engagement, Ralph." He nodded at Patience. "I have only just heard of it."

Ralph could not disguise a slight guiltiness in the smile that followed. "I am very grateful for your good wishes, Edgar. I do feel myself lucky beyond my merits. Miss Emma Marlow is a very patient and a very generous creature, and I admire her more than I can say." Then, a twinkle in his eye, and his old, caustic self won out. "Above all, I think I must applaud her good taste in choosing me."

Edgar laughed, but now without pain; and together the brothers and Patience went in to greet their parents.

Such was the general effusiveness over Ralph—Mrs. Willmot briefly crying over him, and Mr. Willmot telling him that his engagement was "the first thing you've done in which I can find no fault"—that Edgar was quite overlooked. He could not but see this as a blessing; for he had not parted well with his father; there had been sharp words that Edgar blushed later to recall, and he had not known how he should be received.

But Ralph's engagement not only forestalled any confrontation, it so lightened the mood that Mr. Willmot was seen to smile for eleven consecutive minutes—something entirely unprecedented. He even shook Edgar's hand and courteously (though not warmly) welcomed him home.

"My fiancée has asked me," Ralph said after they had all taken seats and been furnished with a drink (port for the gentlemen, madeira for the ladies), "that news of our engagement be kept *en famille* for the time being. She does not wish its publication to draw attention from her sister's nuptials."

"We shall tell no one," Patience assured him.

"I thank you," he said; "that will somewhat atone for my telling everyone." They all laughed, but Ralph insisted that he was being quite candid. "I cannot help it; I know myself. I am no more capable of keeping a secret of this nature than I am of scaling the walls like a gibbon."

"I hope," said Mrs. Willmot with a sly smile, "that by this time next year we shall indeed *have* some sweet gibbons making the attempt."

"Good God, Mrs. Willmot, of what do you speak?" asked her husband, whose wits were now rather dampened by port.

"I mean babies, of course," she said. "With a spring wedding, there is just time for Ralph and his bride to produce one for Christmas next; and if they are lucky, as we were with Mary-Anne and Lucy-Anne, they might manage two."

"Your thoughts run too swiftly, my dear," he replied. "You do better to keep pace with the rest of us, who yet consider no more than the wedding itself."

"But what is a wedding for," she insisted, "if not to pave the way for babies?"

Mr. Willmot looked very much as though he would have liked to answer this; but perhaps thinking better of it, he offered nothing at all.

In the pocket of silence that ensued, Patience—and of course it must be Patience—recalled that Edgar was in the room as well, and moved to include him in the conversation. "And Edgar, what of you? How fare your literary pursuits? And how do you find life at Oxford?"

Mr. Willmot made a great, grumbling noise in his chest that momentarily delayed Edgar's reply; but then he said, "My literary project proceeds apace, sister, and I thank you for the inquiry. As for life at Oxford, it is very lonely at present; but I have great hopes for an improvement, as I have just learned I am to be nominated for a fellowship at my old college."

"That is good news indeed," said Mrs. Willmot with a rather tepid show of enthusiasm.

Mr. Willmot released another gaseous growl, then rose from his chair. "I feel an attack of dyspepsia," he said. "If you will excuse me, I will have Hastings deliver me to bed. Good night to you all."

Edgar felt the slight as keenly as if his father had hurled a paperweight at him; and while the rest of his family strove valiantly to keep their reunion going, it soon dissolved into guilt, mortification, and dismay.

Mr. Redmond had no kin in Marlhurst, and lived alone in rented rooms on Jasper Street. For this reason, coincident with his recent increased intimacy with the Nesmiths, it had become a usual thing for him to stay to dinner on those days when he came to confer with the parson; and afterward he and Alice would sit and talk for an hour or so, while Mr. Nesmith busied himself in his study.

But tonight Alice would have none of that. After the meal she donned her cape and stole from the house, unseen by Green as she cleared the table; and she resolved to stay out of doors until Mr. Redmond had gone home. It would seem very curious that she were not there awaiting him when he and her father came out of the dining room; but they would not be so bold as to search for her. And if they did, they would not find her.

Edgar and Emma

It was rather a reckless thing to do, not only because the night air was very cold—her breath tumbled out of her the way smoke fell from her father's lips when he was at his pipe—but because she risked being seen. As a parson's daughter, she was meant to be not merely respectable but the very model of respectability for the other young ladies of the village; and lurking out of doors under the moonlight did not tally with any definition of respectability she had yet known.

But it seemed that destiny had driven her to such daring, for she was in fact seen—and by he whom she would most have chosen to be her discoverer. One moment she was alone, and wondering whether she had waited long enough to ensure Mr. Redmond's departure; the next, Bravo from Willmot Lodge had turned by the hedge onto the lane, and taken her by surprise; and then, even as Alice held her breath, Edgar Willmot followed, his stride so purposeful that he was very nearly upon her before he saw her.

"Oh! Miss Nesmith," he said. "Good evening. Come, Bravo! To me, Bravo!"

Bravo had been bothering the hem of Alice's cape, and though she tried to move him aside with her foot, she made it out to be nothing. "He does not disturb me," she said. "I am always happy to see him. Hello, Bravo! How does my furry love?"

Edgar approached, grabbed Bravo's collar, and tugged him slightly away. He and Alice were now very near to each other.

"I had not heard that you were come home," Alice said pleasantly.

"I arrived but a few hours past. I am afraid my long journey agitated me, so that I could not sleep; I am hoping to tire myself out with a walk." He scrutinized her as best he could, in the wan light. "And you? Ought you to be out so late? It is well past the dinner hour."

"We often dine late at the parsonage," she said, "which is perhaps not entirely advisable. In fact I felt flush tonight, and have availed myself of the fresh air to drive it from me."

"I think the cure may be more harmful than the complaint," he said; and indeed Alice felt her lips trembling. "Let me escort you to your door."

"You are very kind," she said, slipping from her perch atop the fence that bordered the lane. "But it is only a few steps; and I would be ashamed to take you from your errand."

"My errand, as I have said, is merely to exhaust myself, and I may do that in any direction I choose." He extended his arm.

She took it; but as she did so, she noted the haunted look on his face. "Mr. Willmot," she cried, stopping him after only a few steps, "I hope all is well at the Lodge!"

He daubed swiftly at his eyes, as though the trace of tears there had betrayed him and must be eliminated at once. "All is very well indeed. Today my brother Ralph…" His voice trailed off; it seems he could not complete the sentence.

"I have heard the news," she said with an attempt at brightness. "I wish them both every joy."

He looked at her—more directly and in greater earnest than he ever had, even when he had been a regular caller—and said, "Your generosity does you credit. I wish I could take your example. But I find myself very vexed by the capricious nature of fate. It seems to me so unlikely that two people who wish to come together should ever find the right circumstances in which to do so, that it is a miracle anyone ever comes together at all."

"And yet," Alice said very gently, "here we are."

He seemed to search for a reply to this; and Alice was content to wait as long as required to hear it.

But the fate Edgar had so recently disparaged now proved his case against it by bringing Mr. Nesmith onto the scene.

"Alice," he said, "come into the house."

Edgar, who had started at the sound of the parson's voice—as though he had been caught out in some desperate act—quickly collected himself and said, "Good evening, sir. I was just escorting her to your door."

He narrowed his eyes and said, "So I see," in a tone of voice that clearly implied he saw something quite different. "I thank you, but you need trouble yourself no further."

Edward bowed and departed; Bravo trotted happily behind him.

Mr. Nesmith turned, and gestured for Alice to do the same. As they walked back to the house, he said, "What wantonness was this?"

Alice felt herself color. "None, sir; I felt flush, and went out for some air. Mr. Willmot came upon me unexpectedly. You will recall that he and I are friends."

"And how many 'friends' do you entertain in this manner?" he said with a sneer.

She felt his distrust like a blow, and her voice betrayed her emotion. "It was an innocent encounter, and a singular one," she said. "I beg you, do not mortify me by suggesting otherwise. I am your daughter."

He looked abashed; and as they mounted the steps to the door he said, "I could not find you; I heard voices from without; I investigated. I am sorry to have allowed my surprise to color my judgment."

"And I am sorry that my own judgment was lacking," she replied. "I will be more alert to appearances henceforth."

They went inside; and no more was said of the matter.

But the fright that the parson had suffered—the sudden fear that lasciviousness had spread its influence into his own home and hearth—could not be shaken so easily. He had felt the walls close in on him, seeing Alice outside, under the stars, with a young man; and even after the young man had been revealed as the upright young son of his patron, and Alice's conduct absolved, the walls had not moved back.

And Mr. Nesmith suspected he knew why. It was because today, he had relaxed his own judgment in the interest of kindness and mercy; and now he was plagued by regret and self-doubt.

For today he had baptized a natural child—the newborn son of Violet Cutler.

CHAPTER TWENTY

Tom Peake shook off the cold as he entered The Copper Fox. He craved a cup of mulled wine to warm his bones, over which a chill had settled, traveling on horseback as he was.

The hour was very late and the house was near empty. He did not expect to find a familiar face, and yet there was one seated figure, the back of whose head seemed familiar to him. He moved to where he could obtain a quarter-profile view; and yes—there was no doubt. That chin could not be mistaken. "Willmot!" he called out as he approached. "What an unexpected surprise. And what an age it's been since I've seen you! I hope you will not disdain to speak to me now that I am a Cambridge man."

Edgar turned to face him fully, and Tom's jollity died in his throat; for his old friend and neighbor looked utterly haunted.

"Tom Peake!" Edgar said with a lamentable attempt at a smile. "Of course I will speak to you. Sit down."

Tom sat, and as he did so he decided on a course of frankness, lest Edgar's fragile appearance frighten him into excessive politeness. "I am glad of it; for I think it would do you well to speak to *somebody*."

Edgar looked vastly surprised. "Why do you say so?"

"Your aspect," said Tom. "You are very gaunt; forgive me for saying it, but you seem quite actively oppressed."

Edgar turned back to his tankard and idly stroked its sides. "It is nothing," he said.

"I am glad to hear I am mistaken," said Tom, as he signaled across the room for service. "Perhaps we may ride to Marlhurst together, and become reacquainted." He turned briefly to the barman who had come to attend him, and ordered his mulled wine. When he turned back, he found Edgar's features even more bleakly arranged.

"Alas, we cannot ride together," he said.

Tom leaned back in his chair. "Come, now! You betray your prejudice. You will speak to a Cambridge man, but not ride with him? What manner of distinction is that?"

Edgar shook his head. "You misunderstand me. We cannot ride together, for we our roads lead us apart."

Tom shook his head. "You mean…you do not make for Sussex, from Oxford?"

"No; I return to Oxford, from Sussex."

"You do not stay for Chrismas, then?" said Tom, confused. "Or my sister's wedding?"

Edgar laughed. "Neither. But it does not signify; I will not be missed."

A worrying feeling gripped Tom. He remembered Edgar as being the quieter and more subtle of the elder Willmot brothers; but he did not recall a tendency to dejection.

"I am sure you will be missed very much," he said.

Edgar shook his head. "My father does not speak to me. I do not say he has no cause; but it is a hard thing to bear."

Tom frowned. "Edgar, please attend me: I have lost one father, and been lucky enough to find another in Sir Godfrey. I pray you do not discard your own so hastily. It is a thing you will regret."

"It is not merely my father," Edgar said; "I have forgotten country manners. I know not how to conduct myself."

Edgar and Emma

His eyes met Tom's. "Just prior to my departure, I came very close to shaming an innocent maiden."

Tom's frown deepened. "I think perhaps you make much of what was very likely a small offense."

"No, I assure you; I put a young girl at risk of dishonor —and I did it without a thought. Had we been discovered by any but her father, I tremble to consider the consequences; and even that gentleman's censure will not be easy for her to bear."

Tom grew inquisitive. "Of which young lady do we speak?"

"I must not say," said Edgar, taking up his tankard again. He took a long, slow swallow.

Tom's mind was working. "You do not mean my sister, Emma?"

Edgar nearly choked at this; but recovered and said, "No, no. She is safe from me. She is promised to my brother Ralph."

"Ah," thought Tom. "We begin to get to the meat of the matter."

"You mean to say, Emma is to marry Mr. Ralph Willmot?" he asked.

Edgar nodded as he daubed his mouth with a napkin.

Tom sighed; he knew not what to say. In one sense he felt a pall of guilt, for Emma had confided in him, many months before, her hopes of attaching Edgar; and here was news that she had succeeded, but with the wrong brother. Ought Tom to have given Edgar—or at least Ralph—some intelligence of Emma's preference for the elder of the two, before he had left Marlhurst for Cambridge? But Emma had not granted him liberty to do so; and he would not have thought to ask her for it.

It seemed to him a wonder that the people he had left behind in summer had so mismanaged themselves in the months he had been away. And yet lacking any real understanding of what had occurred, he scrupled to divulge any confidences now.

"And how does Emma's intended suit her?" he asked.

Edgar, still eyeing his tankard, shrugged. "I cannot say; I have not seen her."

"Not even to offer your congratulations?"

By the way Edgar flinched, Tom understood this to mean that it would have been a torment to him to do so. But that did not signify; and Edgar must see as much.

"It will not do for you to be known to have come home to the Lodge," he told him, "and then to have departed it without paying your respects to your brother's bride-to-be. It would convey a grievous disrespect."

Edgar turned his head completely away from Tom; during which time Tom's mulled wine was set before him. He took a sip, felt its gratifying warmth spread through his chest and limbs, then set the cup down and said, "Willmot. I asked you to hear me."

"And I do," said Edgar.

"Come back to Marlhurst with me. Face your disputes and disappointments with a glad heart and a mild manner. All will be well. I am certain of it."

Edgar's shoulders slumped. "You shame me."

"I do not mean to." He checked the clock against the far wall. "It is not yet half-past six o'clock. You must have left the Lodge very early."

"Just after four," Edgar said.

"And you bade no one farewell?"

"I thought it best to take my leave quietly."

Edgar and Emma

"I know you are no coward, Willmot; but you do your best to persuade me otherwise." He took another mouthful from his cup. "It seems a fair guess that if we ride back at once, you may arrive before anyone realizes you are gone. This brief panic can be forgotten, and you may begin to repair the relationships you have strained."

Edgar ran his hand through his hair. "It is kind of you to advise me so; but it is very wrong of me to have given you cause. I am ashamed to have burdened you with so many of my troubles."

"It is perhaps less a reflection on your judgment than on your thirst," said Tom, with an accusatory nod at Edgar's tankard. *"In vino veritas."*

Edgar smiled. "That is clever; but I do not drink wine. This is beer."

"In cerevesio felicitas," Tom shot back.

Edgar laughed. "You are too cunning for me, Peake. I surrender myself to you. Do with me what you will."

"You know what I will," Tom said, and he drained his cup. "Leave with me now, and ride back with me to Marlhurst. And in two days' time, shake my hand at my sister's wedding."

Some few hours later, Emma rose; and after a troubled sleep, she found consciousness no more comforting.

Jenny had come in and opened the curtains just as usual, and helped her to dress; but whatever slight companionability Emma had nurtured between them since her return to Graftings, seemed utterly gone. Her lady's maid had grown measurably more withdrawn over the prior weeks, but today the difference was unmistakable; she was brisk and businesslike, responded to Emma's friendly entreaties with barely audible responses, and fled—there was no other word for it; she would have knocked over anyone unlucky enough to bar her path—as soon as it was permissible to do so.

Hicks had altered as well, beginning with the previous day, when she had offered distinctly pro forma congratulations to Emma on her engagement. Emma had rather dreaded submitting herself to the housekeeper's unchecked volubility, and was amazed to find herself so swiftly dispensed with; though strangely, she could find no com-fort in it.

Her family afforded no greater cheer. Emma had urged them all not to make much of her engagement to Ralph, but to defer all such attention and celebration until after the nuptials of Frances and Mr. Denham, and they now bitterly disappointed her by doing exactly as she asked. Throughout the morning and on into the afternoon, Frances was everything, and Emma entirely forgotten.

Emma began to wonder whether she had acted too much in haste, accepting Ralph's proposal—even encouraging him to offer it—after having refused him twice. Her expectation that the simple fact of being affianced would transform her life into a series of rosy tableaux was not being met. Had she not allowed sufficient time? Would another day do the trick—another week?

Seeking reassurance, she sought out her mother. "Mama, what was it like for you, when you were engaged to Papa? Before you were married, I mean."

Lady Marlow, whom Emma had interrupted while in the act of arranging a bowl of winter flowers, put down a handful of hellebores and furrowed her brow in thought. "Oh, my; that is a very long time to recollect. I believe it was spring when your father did me the honor of requesting my hand; though it may have been late fall. Or high summer. I distinctly remember the sun was in the sky; but the sun is always in the sky, so that does not signify. I recall that my father and mother were very glad of the match; though I think my father had some strong objections. And my mother I believe thought I might do better. We were very much feted, as I recall; though I cannot in truth summon forth any details, and it may be that no one entertained us at all. Your father was a very private young man in those days; though he very much enjoyed company. Oh, it was a time I will never forget! Though I am sorry to confess I do not remember much of it."

This provided Emma little in the way of consolation; and she felt an even greater need of such when she heard from Tom—who was newly arrived from Cambridge—that Edgar was at Willmot Lodge. Emma had not expected him; there had been a feeling of finality about his departure for Oxford in September, including—so Aunt Curtis had implied in a whisper—a very acrimonious breach with his father. And Ralph had never mentioned Edgar coming home for the holiday. Though Ralph, it must be admitted, seldom mentioned anyone but himself.

The idea that she must soon see Edgar—meet him in company; look at him; speak to him—gave her a very queer feeling that she could not reason away. It had been close to a year since the Marlows had returned to Graftings, and in all that time she had not spoken to Edgar in any substantial fashion but twice: once on the churchyard green, and once at the dance. Why was it, then, that the full text of each of those conversations was indelibly etched into her memory, whereas her glib and easy exchanges with Ralph from any of his recent visits dissolved in the air the moment he took his leave of her? She could no more recall what they had spoken of yesterday than she could lead an army into battle, or bake a cake.

With a great summoning of will, she reminded herself of how grown-up she had felt in accepting Ralph; how proud she had been that she had made a choice without any illusions—had made it while recognizing that there would be difficulties and incongruities connected to it. This problem of Edgar must be one of them. And so she resolved to face it bravely, and to endure it by employing the full complement of her powers.

She would succeed in this. She would; indeed, she *must*.

CHAPTER TWENTY-ONE

The day of the wedding found Mr. Nesmith yet in an ill humor. He had been unable to relinquish the suspicion that his generosity of spirit had been used against him, and that as a result he had allowed wickedness to triumph.

There was, admittedly, scant evidence to support such a claim; in fact he chose not to mention the matter to Alice, as he knew she should point out how much he made of so little. But he had learned to trust his instincts, and these were now in a state of unified aggrievement.

He had made no secret of his conviction that Violet Cutler, the disgraced housemaid, should be forgiven her transgression and not ostracized by the village's Christian community; and he had accordingly agreed to her request that the child of her folly be baptized into that community —to which Mr. Nesmith saw no objection, as the child himself bore no fault in the matter.

But he had expected that Violet would acknowledge his magnanimity by conducting herself with appropriate humility and submission; that she would honor his forgiveness of her shame by demonstrating her own conviction that she was unworthy of such largesse. To him, it was almost a contract between God and sinner that the former might absolve the latter, but the latter must never absolve herself.

And at first Violet had seemed in accord with this precept; indeed it had been her longstanding wretchedness that had moved him to pity in the first place. Even before the child was born, she had been bereft in contemplation of its soul. Thus she had answered Mr. Nesmith's offer with gratifying modesty and even a few dignified tears, and had conducted herself very quietly and respectfully during the ceremony itself.

But once the service was concluded and the child returned to her, and the congregants stepped away from the font and out onto the church green, Violet's manner underwent a distressing metamorphosis; suddenly she was merry, her face lit with joy—and she and several of her intimates even joked and laughed with one another.

Mr. Nesmith was shocked; it was his view that no one in Violet Cutler's place had any cause for laughter, ever. He could only surmise that she had deliberately masked her scandalous irreverence until she had got what she wanted from him; which was, her child's salvation. And now that she had it, she cared nothing for his good opinion.

The idea that he had been so easily deceived rendered Mr. Nesmith suspicious of everyone around him, from his farthest-flung parishioners to the daughter under his own roof. How many of them put on a special face just for him —adopted in his presence a demeanor designed specifically for his benefit, which they later shirked like a burdensome yoke?

Every smile he had encountered since—every pair of merry eyes, every how-do-you-do, every sound of distant laughter—seemed to him part of a conspiracy to hide from him the reality of life in Marlhurst, which was both venal and carnal, and wholly self-loving.

It was in this frame of mind that he donned his cassock and surplice and made ready to officiate the wedding ceremony.

Edgar and Emma

"We are gathered here on this day, to join this man and this woman in holy wedlock, as consecrated by God," said Mr. Nesmith; "that being the solitary state established for mankind, in which he may explore his passions without restraint. And I commend these two young people, come before us in all their freshness and innocence"—and here all looked at elderly Mr. Denham, who was seen to blush; indeed this was perhaps the only thing that could be said of him that *would* make him blush—"for they have resisted the temptation to yield to their baser natures, so that their union might be of the highest and most exemplary kind." At this, Mr. Denham audibly giggled.

Tom had never heard Mr. Nesmith deliver a nuptial sermon, and he was momentarily taken aback by the admonishing nature of it—as though all who heard it, save the two paragons who were its fountainhead, were the foulest of animals. And yet, on reflection, Tom did not see why celebrating a wedding should cause any material modification in the parson's manner. His thundering style was a fixed thing, impervious to outside influences; indeed, the fact of a wedding seemed almost tacked on to the address —barely considered, as if insufficiently worthy of the parson's notice. Certainly he had taken no close look at Mr. Denham.

"Our ardent suitor," Mr. Nesmith continued, "thus with angelic grace claims the maidenhead of his bride, and spares her the impurity of ill use—of serving merely as a vessel for the fulfillment of sordid desires, of the kind we see everywhere around us in these degraded times—yes, *everywhere!* Look about you, sinners: for on every side, you are hemmed in by the lecherous, the iniquitous, the unclean!"

Tom did indeed take the suggestion to look around him; but it was not evidence of debauchery he sought. He was seated in the front row with the Marlows and the Curtises —as befitted the family of the bride—and had been watching to gauge Emma's response to meeting Edgar again. But she had skillfully avoided him thus far; and Tom saw now that she made no attempt even to look across the aisle to where he sat with his own, more extensive family. Edgar himself was not so strong-willed, for Tom several times caught him in the act of glancing over at Emma; and so did Ralph. Which might, Tom reflected, explain why Emma kept her own gaze fixed solidly ahead; she did not wish mistakenly to meet the eyes of one brother, in an attempt to fix on the other.

"For this I promise you," Mr. Nesmith declaimed, his tone rising in pitch as his text swelled in indignation, "this plague of turpitude, of intemperance—this reckless giving over to repeated and scandalous dissipation—it will lead to nothing less than the wholesale destruction of our empire, of our *kind*, in a storm of divine retribution, leaving us—*all* of us—broken and ravaged, and not sated but despairing, the flesh which we so wantonly corrupted, now corrupt in every manner: falling slack from our bones, stinking and decayed, to infect and poison the God-forsaken earth."

Mr. Nesmith had reached such a crescendo of wrath that the lectern itself visibly wobbled from the vibrations of his voice. But now he broke off, and after tossing a look of disgust at the congregation, turned away from them and onto the steps that led back down to the altar. A moment later he disappeared behind the pulpit.

The assembly waited patiently for him to re-emerge; but after several moments he had not done so so—and Tom found himself wondering if, in his absence, the church had been so renovated that now the steps extended deep beyond the church's floor, and Mr. Nesmith was descending them into the bowels of the earth.

After a few moments more, open murmuring began, and Tom—being nearest the pulpit—slipped out of the pew and went to investigate; arriving just as the verger did, from the back of the church.

They found Mr. Nesmith in a heap at the bottom of the steps, his mouth working as though to call for help, but no sound emerging. Tom and Mr. Redmond took one arm each and got him to his feet; and once he was upright he seemed to regain some clarity of speech. But he was still very unsteady and occasionally unintelligible, so that Tom and the verger had to help him through the remainder of the ceremony. But there was no question that Frances and Mr. Denham exited the church as man and wife, and since that was all that really mattered, the apprehensions and inelegancies of the service were soon forgotten.

That is, they were forgotten by all but Alice and the verger, who managed between them to get Mr. Nesmith home and into bed, where over the next several hours his condition worsened; and so a physician was summoned.

Emma's impulse on returning to Graftings was to flee to her room; not for the rest of her life, but only long enough to recover her composure from having seen Edgar. But the Marlows were accompanied by a small party of guests from other counties, and it would be rude for Emma so plainly to abandon them; so she chose instead to slip away quietly before entering the house, and to find the solitude she desired in a walk.

Alas, the grounds were thick with yew trees and very uneven, so that she could not ramble as she might have liked, but must follow the sole path worn into the earth by those many (including herself) who had discovered it as the only safe route over the terrain. And this brought her inevitably to the place where, six years before, she had turned her ankle and seen a snake, and required Edgar's rescue; so that his presence here was not only not undiminished, but more powerful than ever.

She had only required one glance at him, outside the church before the service, to feel in her breast the certainty that she had acted in haste. Edgar looked pale and gaunt and not at all well, and indeed seemed almost ghostly next to the sunny vitality of his brother, whose masculine prowess was such that the very clouds seemed to part for him. And yet for Emma, Ralph was nothing; Edgar was all.

But this epiphany availed her naught; for she had promised herself to Ralph, and even if she could extricate herself from that commitment—which she could not; for what cause could she give?—she would be no nearer to a life with Edgar, who had found her charms so resistible that they had been easily overridden by his desire to live at Oxford, where—she was certain—the memory of Miss Emma Marlow seldom if ever troubled him.

By the time she had concluded her walk—and it had been a long one, for she had had much to think through—she was persuaded that her response to seeing Edgar again was a reason to *prefer* Ralph. For what danger might there be, in loving a man who robbed her of her reason? With Ralph, she need never fear that she would be induced to act against her better nature, or allow him liberties that would injure her in some way—and she knew he would try. There was safety in being wed to a man who could not rule her.

Although that kind of safety was only necessary with a man one could not trust. She laughed to think so, and muttered, "But surely that is any man;" and even as she said it, it sounded harsh and cynical to her ears. For she could not deny that she did trust Edgar; and yet she barely knew him. She must now persuade herself that were she better acquainted with him, she would see this flaw in him as well.

By the time she reentered Grafting the party had dispersed; and in the drawing room she found only her mother and father and Tom, and Mr. Denham.

"There you are!" Lady Marlow said. "Frances has been looking for you, to say good-bye. She and our dear Mr. Denham depart for Waylands."

"Where is she?" Emma asked as she doffed her hat.

"Taking her leave of the staff. She will return forthwith."

But Mr. Denham's nervous fidgeting—he still seemed less than entirely comfortable with Sir Godfrey—agitated the air in the drawing room, so Emma said she would go and find Frances rather than wait for her.

As she made her way down the narrow staircase, she wondered at how seldom she had done so; she could count the occasions easily on the fingers of one hand. And it was a further surprise when she found Frances in the kitchen, in her traveling clothes, all the staff ranged around her—and dawdling a baby in her arms.

At the sight of Emma, the easy companionability of the scene ended; the servants visibly stiffened, and the very air about them turned crisp and chill.

"Frances," she said, "I am glad I did not miss you; I have come to bid you farewell."

Even her sister seemed alarmed to see her; and she handed the baby off—to Violet Cutler; so that Emma now realized that this was the child for whom Violet had suffered so much disgrace. Emma herself would never have thought to inquire after it, much less fondle it.

"Thank you again for all your good wishes," said Frances, shaking Hicks's hand; "I wish you all very well in return."

And then she joined Emma, and led her gently back out to the stairs.

As they ascended, Frances said, "I am very sorry to have put you in that position, Emma; but I did not know you would come down."

Emma was perplexed by this, and said only, "I am not perturbed."

"Violet's sister cares for the child in the village," she said; "but I asked to see it, so she brought it here to the house. It is me you must blame."

"I do not consider it a thing worthy of blame," Emma said, wishing she could see Frances's face; but they were climbing single file, since the stairs were not wide enough to accommodate them two abreast.

"Well, now that you *have* seen it," Frances said with a wry inflection in her voice, "I suppose you can have no doubt. Was that not indeed the Willmot chin?"

Emma stopped on the stairs, just shy of reaching the landing, and stood there, dumbstruck, until Frances—having emerged above and found herself alone—looked back and said, "Emma? What is the matter?"

She found that she could barely speak. With great effort, she said, "Please explain what you mean by that last remark."

Frances furrowed her brow. "Come, Emma—do not toy with me so. You cannot mean to say you do not know."

"Do not know what?" she asked; it emerged as a kind of wail.

"Oh, dear," said Frances; "I forget how adept you can be at living entirely in a world of your own manufacture."

Edgar and Emma

And suddenly, Emma knew. Suddenly it all made sense.

The cautious, brittle manner of the staff whenever Ralph paid a call; the complete alteration in their manner towards her while he courted her, and even more so when she agreed to marry him; Frances's comment that she was "brave to take him on."

"Why did no one tell me?" Emma gasped.

"Why did you not open your eyes?" Frances said. Then she extended her hand: "Come, I do not wish to be unkind. I must leave this house, and I do not expect that you and I will see each other very often from now on; I would not have our final parting as sisters beneath the same roof to be marred by ill feeling."

Emma regained her composure and mounted the final few steps, then enfolded Frances in a fond embrace.

"There is no ill feeling," she said. "Quite the contrary: you have all my love, Frances. And you have as well my gratitude."

CHAPTER TWENTY-TWO

Mrs. Curtis was talking even before she entered Graftings —thinking aloud, as was her wont—and when she stepped into the foyer it was the work of an instant to switch from speaking to herself, to addressing one other—and then another yet.

"—must remind Dobbs to set aside the gold cloth should Lady Marlow—good afternoon, Hicks, I've come to see your mistress—oh, but here is Mr. Peake, I will speak with him first; thank you, Hicks. Well, Tom, now that we have put the wedding behind us, we must look ahead to Christmas; and since you all are used to spend it in Wiltshire, I am worried you will be insufficiently furnished here at Graftings. So I have come to offer you the use of my plate and trimmings, of which I am over-supplied, as I have collected much more than I need, for as you may know Mr. Curtis dislikes to make a fuss of the holiday."

"I thank you for my part," Tom said, "but my foster-mother has instructed that all she required be delivered from Dunfosters. Indeed I believe it has already arrived."

Mrs. Curtis paused in the removal of her gloves, as if uncertain whether she now had cause to complete the operation. "Well, then, that is one errand off my list; I would they were all accomplished so easily." She glanced at the door, as if contemplating returning as she had come in; but after another moment's reflection she grasped Tom's arm and said, "But here is my opportunity to congratulate you on the fine figure you cut at the church yesterday."

He blushed. "I cannot think what you mean."

She squeezed him teasingly. "I think you must. You were the hero of the hour, my dear; the way you swept in and rescued the parson—I confess I found it quite thrilling!"

"I wish I could say I rescued him; but alas, I have heard that he has worsened since the incident. For my part, I did no more than any gentleman would do."

"Ah—but no other gentleman *did*. Only you."

"Well... I and Mr. Redmond."

Mrs. Curtis looked momentarily perplexed, as though the concept of a "Mr. Redmond" were something she had once grasped but since forgotten. Then she recovered and said, "Oh, yes; if you must have it so. But as he is the verger, it could be said that he did no more than his duty."

"That is perhaps uncharitable to him," said Tom gently.

But Mrs. Curtis was too caught up in the momentum of her own thoughts to be deflected by even the mildest rebuke. "I think you must be a hero in particular to Miss Nesmith, who cannot but have suffered such terrors for her father; and how she must have rejoiced to see you take him in hand!"

"I do not think Miss Nesmith is quite capable of rejoicing just yet, aunt. The parson remains very seriously ill."

"Oh, you know what I mean." She squeezed him again. "I am very sure that she realizes that were it not for you, she must have lost him entirely."

"I think that is a vast overstatement." His smile had by now largely wilted. He did not like being made much of; unhappily, it was Mrs. Curtis's chief delight to subject him to it.

"You do not know a woman's mind," she said, drawing him closer. "Neither do not know the extent of a woman's gratitude. But I think soon you must."

He laughed. "Aunt! You are shocking."

"Perhaps I am precipitate; but I cannot help it. I know Miss Nesmith; she is a particular friend of mine. And I have always found her the warmest, most appreciative, dearest girl in the world. And I am certain of what her feelings must be on this occasion. I do not wish to discomfit you, Tom—" ("That ship has long sailed," thought he.) "—but if you had a mind to do so, you would find her quite receptive to your calling at the parsonage. You may position it as an expression of concern for the parson. But I think you will find its chief reward will be the friendship of his charming daughter."

Tom laughed again, but longed to get away; alas, this was impossible until his aunt released her grip on his arm. "I am certain Miss Nesmith is all the things you say she is," he said. "But even were I inclined to seek the favor of your friend, I would not choose to do so now. Her father has suffered a very grievous attack; all her thoughts must be of his recovery."

She waved her free hand in dismissal. "I am certain Mr. Nesmith's improvement will be swift. My husband sits with him even now, and he is sure to see that he mends entirely; no one would dare to cross Mr. Curtis. In the meantime, Tom, let me enlighten you: a woman's thoughts are *never* all of one thing. She is perpetually open to affairs of the heart. Why, this matter of the service you have rendered Miss Nesmith is very like the way in which Mr. Curtis and I were brought together. Have I not told you of our first meeting?"

Edgar and Emma

Tom, who dreaded above all things the stories of how couples came to be, lightly tested his aunt's hold on him; still unyielding. "I cannot recall," he said dejectedly. "Very possibly."

"Well, if you are uncertain, then it bears repeating. I was just sixteen; it was the year of the King's jubilee. You are too young to remember it, Tom; but there were celebrations across the length and breadth of the realm. One such was a great party given here in Marlhurst; there were tables in the street, heaped with pies and meats and hogsheads of beer. And fireworks!—oh, it was such a sight as I have never seen since. I was visiting my brother Baldwin, who was then in residence at Graftings, and thus I was a guest at his table. And as the night wore on, one of the local gentlemen grew very merry from drink and got up onto the table and sang 'Robin Adair' in a very handsome tenor—and not only sang it, but followed with a little jig as well, during which he kicked over a flagon of ale, which landed in Mrs. Lerner's lap and put her decidedly out of temper. For my part, I was charmed by the performance and I asked my uncle who this raucous gentleman might be, and what do you suppose was his answer?—Why, it was Mr. Curtis! I asked to be introduced to him, and within a twelvemonth we were married. You look astonished, Tom; no doubt because you know Mr. Curtis as teetotal. And it is true, he gave up drink once we were wed. Oh, he admits to a periodic inclination to imbibe; but he says I am his deliverance, for one look at me reminds him of the consequences. And this from a man not liberal with his compliments! I am often moved to tears."

A few moments passed in silence; and when it became clear that the narrative had reached its conclusion, Tom said, "That is a very pretty story, aunt; but it bears no resemblance of any kind to Miss Nesmith and me."

Again she looked surprised, as though, having arrived safely in port, she had forgot the harbor she set sail from. "Oh, well—as to that—no, I suppose you are right. Only in that it features Mr. Curtis making himself an object of notice, and my noticing him; which is very much the same as you and Alice."

Tom struggled to keep a grimace from claiming his face. "If you will have it so."

"Oh!" she cried, squeezing him with both hands now, "you are very unromantic! It makes me quite furious. I would have thought the example of a wedding would have pried open your dry, scholar's heart, Tom. But if this one has not, perhaps the one just coming will have better effect."

Tom furrowed his brow. "Which one is that, aunt?"

"Why, Emma and Ralph Willmot's! What other could I mean?"

Tom's face softened. "Ah. Yes. As to that," he said, leading her across the hall to the privacy of a bench in a far corner, "there has been news you have not yet heard…"

Ralph was not in the habit of frequenting Marlhurst's sole tap room. He might debauch himself to any extent he liked abroad, but he took care that his behavior in his home county gave no one cause to complain of him. Any public display of dissipation would ultimately not be worth the temporary enjoyment it might impart.

But he availed himself of the tap room today, for he had been greatly disappointed, and greatly disgusted. He had shamed himself at home, despite his attempts at discretion; and he had been discovered and condemned by the most unfortunate judge of all: the woman he had wished to marry.

In truth, he had almost forgotten Violet Cutler. He had been careless there, to be sure; but the girl had seemed to understand the risks, and made no demands on him when she found herself in distress. Neither had she named Ralph as the co-author of her shame. So Ralph had considered the matter well settled; the parson had even intervened to keep the girl employed at Graftings, so that he need suffer no guilt over her ostracism from the community.

Had he known that, mere months after his folly, the Marlows would return to Graftings, and that he would find in Emma Marlow the woman most suited not only to delivering him from his accumulated troubles, but a woman whom he might come to cherish as much as respect, he would have given Violet Cutler a wide berth; but when the Marlows did indeed reinstall themselves in their ancestral house, Violet had for so long been quiet and acquiescent that Ralph had thought it worth the risk.

Yet somehow, it had all gone wrong. He very early detected a kind of reluctance among the Graftings staff to cater to him too directly; from which he deduced that among her fellow staff, at least, Violet's history was better known. Still he counted on the discretion of the serving class; they tended not to air their grievances, because doing so seldom helped to ease them—and indeed often added to their weight.

But while the servants may have honored convention, their masters had done otherwise. Ralph had not reckoned with the genial slackness of the Marlows; for a baronet's family, they were very casual about relations with those in their employ. Many a time Ralph had witnessed Frances Marlow in happy conference with one or other of the staff, and it was clear to him that the matters under discussion had nothing at all to do with mending pelisses or polishing silver. He had not worried overmuch; Frances, after all, was most often in the company of dogs, and he was perfectly content that she should tell those creatures any of his secrets that she might happen to discover. They at least were famously nonjudgmental; and even were they not— bites heal.

But Frances and Emma were sisters; and what one knew, the other must eventually learn. What a maddening irony that this had occurred the very day Frances had departed Graftings forever; just a few hours more, and Ralph would have been free and clear!

Yet even with the truth revealed, he would not have considered himself utterly lost. His expectation for such a confrontation had involved denunciations, accusations of betrayal, angry tears and angrier words (he had experienced the sharp end of Emma's tongue often enough), and even a breaking off of the engagement. All of these he might have endured, in the hope that later, when tears had dried and passions had abated, he might make amends—heal the breach and restore their amity, leaving them no longer in an innocent idyll, but with a wiser and more forgiving under-standing of each other.

But Emma had surprised him by being cool—almost tranquil. "I am sorry that this has come to my attention," she said after divulging what she had learned. "It is simply not the kind of thing I can countenance in a husband. I fear I allowed Frances's wedding to render me a silly idealist; I am ashamed that you have ended up the victim of such a girlish fancy. I am old enough to have known better."

She was so dispassionate…so unmoved; indeed, it was *she* who apologized to *him*. He found himself wounded to the quick; that someone who had meant to marry him could dispense with him with so little pain! That he was so irrelevant, where he thought he mattered most.

He had done his best to argue her back into accord. "But, my dear Emma—you cannot condemn me for a single lapse!"

"It is but the single lapse I know of," she said with brutal precision, "and that only because it was committed in a house belonging to my family. Can you honestly tell me there have been no others?"

He felt his face burn; he knew not how best to answer. "It is the only one in Marlhurst," he said at last.

She actually laughed at this!—and prettily, too. No other response could have scalded him half so badly. "You do not make favorable case for yourself," she said; "but I thank you for not attempting to lie to me. That would have been very hard to bear."

"But that is all in the past," he vowed; "when we are married, there will be no recurrence of such dissipations."

She raised an eyebrow at him. "Come now, Mr. Willmot; that is not a promise you can make with any confidence. You are well enough acquainted with your character to know as much."

He had told her then—and honestly, too; he had never spoken more earnestly—that her fine qualities had inspired in him the desire to become a better man. "You will be the making of me, Emma! You, and you alone."

At this she had sighed, as though having heard something very childish that she must now endeavor to explain in simple terms. "Shall I tell you how that will end?" she said. "You will strive to adhere to this design, and for a time all will be well; but inevitably you will grow weary of it, or bored, or come upon some opportunity for pleasure before you can erect a guard against it—and then you will succumb. And afterward you will blame me, for not having been your salvation after all. You will grow to despise me, and a deep rift of bitterness and secrets will open up between us."

"No—with your help, with your love, I can be the man you wish me to be!"

She had rung the bell then—summoning Hicks to show him out—and he knew he faced his final dismissal. "Perhaps I am indeed a romantic," she said, "but I hope of a more rational kind. Matrimony, to my way of thinking, only ever stands a chance at happiness if both parties enter into it fully content with each other exactly as they are. If there is some expectation that once the vows are spoken, one or the other will undergo some great change, to the benefit of both…well, I have never known anything of the like to occur, and I have known many married couples. I must look to them for my example. Again, I ask your forgiveness; and I hope that we may continue as the best of friends. Ah, Hicks—Mr. Willmot is just going. Where are my father and mother? Still in the conservatory?—Thank you, Hicks."

And with that, he was escorted to the door, while Emma went, with maddening sangfroid, to tell her parents that she was no longer to be wed.

Ralph had been used to all the world falling under his sway. He enjoyed it; he took pride in seducing those who were initially indifferent to him, and making them his abject admirers. That he had given his heart—and to the extent possible, for one so self-loving, he had—to a woman who had reversed this formula, was not to be borne.

And so…he drank.

Edgar and Emma

And he did not care who saw him; for what future had he in Marlhurst? He would certainly not stay here to be laughed at…to be the subject of merry gossip at every Christmas dinner table. He would leave the village—leave Sussex—forever. Damn the Lodge and damn the family name; he had his cunning, and he had his charm. He would survive; he would *thrive*…

His sodden reverie was interrupted by a local lad. "Mr. Willmot, sir—I beg your pardon; there is a lady outside who asks for you."

A lady—? His first thought was that Emma had found him, and meant to apologize for her earlier dismissal and beg him to have her back. But no; that was very unlike her; and even if she were so minded, she would reverse herself again on discovering that he was to be found in the murky recesses of the tap room.

But if not Emma, who? He got to his feet somewhat unsteadily, straightened his jacket, and with as much gravity as he could muster, went outside.

Mrs. Curtis awaited him; and the moment she set eyes on him, she came at him in a great rush of feeling. "Oh, my dear Mr. Willmot, I am so glad I have found you! I am sore distraught by what I have heard. I beg you not to give yourself over to hopelessness; I am certain that I can persuade Emma to see what a terrible mistake she has made! She has always been such a proud girl; but she is not insensible to reason. She must be made to forgive you—she *will* forgive you; gentlemen *must* be forgiven their indiscretions, or what would become of society?"

"I thank you, ma'am," Ralph replied, doing his best to mask the telling laziness of his vowels, "but if, as you say, Emma is proud, I am prouder; and I will not become anyone's supplicant, especially someone who, as you say, ought to be better acquainted with the workings of the world."

He made to reenter the tap room, but she grasped his hand and held it fast. It was a very daring thing to do, and it made him look at her in a new light.

"I cannot bear it," she said; "you are too fine to suffer such injury; I will not allow the world to blemish your perfection. You must let me be your champion! Give me leave, and I will restore everything to you. I do not know how I will manage it…but you must let me try. You must… you must…" And here, her eyes welled with earnest, urgent tears.

Since childhood, Ralph had known a thrilling temptation, one with which he occasionally flirted but never entirely embraced; it was the urge, sometimes nearly overwhelming, to smash everything. What must that feel like? To take one's arm and sweep away all the carefully constructed scaffolding of one's life, dashing it to bits, and not give a thought to what came after?

As he looked now into the tear-stained eyes—the very *pretty* tear-stained eyes—of the one creature in all the world who had not disdained or discarded or despised him—who, quite the contrary, still regarded him worshipfully—who quite plainly adored him—Ralph thought perhaps the time had come to find out how it felt.

And to see, at long last, what came after.

CHAPTER TWENTY-THREE

"I beg your pardon, my lady," said Mrs. Hicks, "I was wondering whether you would still be six for dinner."

"Oh, I'm sorry, Hicks—no. I should have let you know, but with one thing and another...alas." She shook her head sadly, then looked up and said, "Mr. Willmot will no longer be joining us."

"And Mrs. Curtis?"

"Mrs. Curtis will be here as planned." Something about the housekeeper looked skeptical, so Lady Marlow added, "What is it, Hicks? Why do you ask?"

"Forgive me, my lady; only William the page—who was on an errand for Mr. Samson—he came back and says to me—well, let me just say that William is a very honest lad, I've never known him to tell a falsehood, nor even to exaggerate the truth; he speaks plainly is my meaning—only he will take forever to get to a point, so as you find yourself wanting to give him a good shake, and say, 'Out with it!'— and you may be sure I've tried many a time to cure him of the habit, but he will persist in it, which is a wonder to me, because he has my good example as well as all the others hereabout; but all this is just to reassure you that William's word may be trusted, when he came back from his errand —the one for Mr. Samson as I mentioned earlier—and says to me that he saw Mrs. Curtis leaving the village."

Lady Marlow set down the tambour on which she was working a scene of a stag being torn apart by hounds. "I expect she has merely gone to Willmot Lodge," she said.

"That's just what I says to William, my lady—only he tells me—and again I reassure you, never a lie from that boys lips; though often times he will say nothing when he ought to do otherwise, and haven't I told him that to hold back a truth is as good as a lie; though I have little hope that he has learned this lesson as yet—though he is very young and I am sure of his good sense in the long run—but William says to me that Mrs. Curtis was not on foot, but in a coach."

Lady Marlow turned in her chair to give the housekeeper her full attention. "And was Mr. Curtis with her?"

Hicks looked suddenly abashed. "No, my lady."

A silence fell between them; which Lady Marlow must eventually break by saying, "Well, who then, Hicks? For I daresay she was not on her own."

The housekeeper looked as though she would rather hide under her own skirts than say what must be said. "She was with Mr. Willmot, my lady."

By the following morning the couple's flight was, by some peculiar village alchemy, known to everyone. Mrs. Curtis would have been humbled to know that despite her many efforts to dispense news to her neighbors hither and yon with as much alacrity as her slender feet would allow, this particular bulletin spread just as swiftly without her—and arguably with fewer distortions of fact. Everyone now knew that Emma had broken off her engagement with Ralph, and why; they knew as well that Ralph had taken to the tap room to console himself, and that Mrs. Curtis had trailed him there, and that afterwards they had set off together. The one thing no one knew, was where they had gone.

At Graftings, there had been one dreadful moment when, on hearing the news, Sir Godfrey had said to his daughter, "Had you not refused him, Emma, this would never have occurred," and Emma so far forgot her duty to her father that she apologized for not having done him the honor of giving him a profligate and a seducer for a son-in-law, before fleeing up to her room for the rest of her life. But passionate feelings soon abated, amends were made, and the family was restored to the kind of solidarity they would require if they were to survive the crisis.

At the Lodge, Mrs. Willmot was chiefly occupied by trying to keep the unfortunate news from any of her younger children, though David must of course hear it on his many rounds among the tenants. Mr. Willmot took to his library and forbade any intrusion on his privacy there; he was so shamed by his son's perfidy that he could not endure the sight of another human face, whether its aspect were angry or (perhaps even worse) condolatory.

The most composed response was that of Mr. Curtis, who when told of where and with whom his wife had last been seen, said, "I think we need not discompose the Willmots with excessive questions on the matter; there can be little mistaking the objective." His only inquiry was whether the coach in which the pair had fled had been hired for the purpose; he loathed to think that Ralph might have stolen one from the Lodge's stable on his wife's behalf.

The coach was later found to have been hired; but other crimes were suspected, and much discussed among the villagers. Mrs. Treacher wondered whether Ralph had put Mrs. Curtis in similar straits to those in which he had landed Violet Cutler, and Mrs. Barret speculated that Ralph had abducted Mrs. Curtis in revenge for having discovered that the Marlows, of whose fortune he had planned to avail himself once married to Emma, were in fact penniless. Each day brought a new report of Mrs. Willmot falling into a swoon and breaking her head, or of Tom Peake challenging Ralph to a duel, or of Mrs. Curtis's earthly remains being discovered in Gatwick Stream. In short, the villagers had not so thoroughly enjoyed a Christmas week in many a year; and most cheerful of all was Madame Claude, from whose head was finally lifted the burden of being the most despised person in Marlhurst. So effectively had Ralph Willmot replaced her, she had even been forgiven by her erstwhile archenemy, Mrs. Heath, who with great magnanimity actually entered the drapery and purchased a satin waistcoat for her husband's Christmas gift. Madame Claude, who had learned her lesson, charged her but eleven shillings.

Such general merriment at the expense of the neighborhood's leading families cannot be expected have been shared by them, and indeed Christmas looked to be a very glum occasion for the Willmots and the Marlows, especially since their society with each other had ceased out of mutual mortification. Mrs. Willmot and Lady Marlow had exchanged notes of consolation and fellow-feeling, but the undercurrents of guilt and ignominy which could be obscured in a few lines of text, would be impossible to conceal in any more substantial congress.

Mr. Curtis, cuckolded and abandoned, had been invited to Christmas dinner at Graftings; but he sent his regrets, declaring instead his intention to pass that holiest of evenings comforting his friend Mr. Nesmith—who was in much dismay that his infirmity would prevent him delivering the Christmas sermon over which he had labored so long. (Intelligence of Mr. Curtis's own plight had been kept from the parson; given that extreme agitation on the theme of carnal misconduct had brought on Mr. Nesmith's seizure, it was thought that news of Ralph Willmot and Mrs. Curtis's elopement might trigger a relapse—if not his actual demise.)

For the next few days, Edgar was greatly occupied by consoling his father and mother; as was Emma with hers. There was little chance of them meeting, though both longed for—and at the same time dreaded—the day such a reunion would be possible.

The opportunity presented itself on the morning of the twenty-second, when David was helping one of the Willmot tenants, Mr. Fry, build a temporary windbreak for his cattle in anticipation of the nights getting colder. A traveling tradesman, Mr. Ivy, who passed often through Marlhurst, stopped to observe their work; and when he recognized David, he happily informed him that his brother, Mr. Ralph Willmot, was in excellent health, as he had shared an ale with him two nights past, just south of Birmingham.

"He has abandoned her," said Edgar when David told the family what he had learned. "The Marlows must be told."

And rather than commit the awful intelligence to paper, Edgar undertook to ride over to Graftings and convey the evil tidings himself.

The Marlows bore the news with all the fortitude one would expect in a titled family; though it was evident that Mrs. Curtis's plight was a great worry to them. They even managed a heroic show of benevolence when Edgar conveyed his own personal apologies for his brother's mischief, by not only dismissing any notion of Edgar's culpability in the matter, but by insisting he stay for dinner as well.

"You need not concern yourself with dress," said Lady Marlow, "for under the circumstances we observe no ceremony."

"You are very kind," he said with a bow, "but I would not intrude upon your grief."

"It is for that very purpose I have asked you," she said with a melancholy smile. "We grow weary of our own sad faces at table, and the diversion of a new countenance, even one as doleful as our own, would be a great relief to us."

Edgar could not but accept; indeed it was his pleasure to do so, for though Emma spoke not a word, he fancied he could feel her urging him not to go away. When the interview ended, the Marlows' valet, Samson, took him upstairs where he might refresh himself; and when he had done so he emerged to find Emma waiting in the corridor.

"Let me not alarm you," she said; "my design is only to commend you for having braved a bitter day to bring us equally bitter news. You are a better friend to us than any other; and I hope that we may be so to you as well. For our families suffer equally in this, I think."

"You are very kind to apportion blame so democratically," he said with a winsome smile, "when you know full well how persuasive my brother can be, and how credulous your aunt."

She seemed to want to laugh, but would not let herself, given the gravity of their mutual plight. Yet the desire shone in her eyes, and infected him with a sudden lightness. For this, she seemed very wonderful to him.

"I daresay all will be well," he offered; "for we are Christian folk, and must excuse the transgressions of our fellow men and women, as we would ourselves be pardoned."

"I think that will be the easiest feature of our present drama," she said as she turned to lead him down the stairs. "Far more challenging is this terrible waiting; how it drains one's strength! We cannot act until we know more; and we cannot know when such intelligence may come."

It came even as she spoke of it. William the page had returned from the village, where he had collected the latest post; which, on inspection, was found to include a letter from Frances.

CHAPTER TWENTY-FOUR

The arrival of a missive from the eldest Marlow daughter caused a considerable stir, as Frances was a famously indifferent correspondent; she was also on her honeymoon, which seemed the least likely time she would choose to amend this fault.

Sir Godfrey read the letter aloud.

My dear Mama and Papa,

We have stopped in town because I have always wanted to see it, but Mr. Denham cannot show it to me as he is so tired from traveling that he must sleep all day, though how he manages I am sure I do not know for the noise here is infernal. I have had to go out on my own and with no one to guide me or advise me I can say only that I find London both very inspiring and very alarming. Chipping Norton is nothing to it.

But I write chiefly to say that while I passed through a place called Charing Cross, I caught sight of my Aunt Curtis. I did not at first believe it could be she, but when I called out her name she turned at once, and looked very sorry to see me; indeed she fled before I could approach.

She appeared very pitiable and I cannot imagine what has happened in Marlhurst where after all I have only been absent three days. But I thought you ought to know what I have seen.

If you have any scraps left from the kitchen I would consider it a kindness if you would have them wrapped and sent to Waylands for the dogs. They are accustomed to it from Mr. Denham and me but I do not imagine the staff provides the same courtesy, indeed I expect they may be jealous of the scraps.

Fondly
FRANCES DENHAM

The sensation this caused—and the variety of emotions it prompted—I leave you to imagine. But its ultimate effect was to galvanize the families into taking action. Now that Mrs. Curtis had been pinpointed on the map of Britain, a search would be undertaken; the only question was, who would go.

Mr. Curtis was the first appealed to; a message was sent to him while the family dined, and its reply arrived before they had finished:

"I do not see the sense in my endeavoring to find my wife," he wrote, "What if I were successful? She disdained to obtain my permission to leave; for which reason I must conclude she would think little of my admonition to return."

"Then you must go, Sir Godfrey," said Lady Marlow. When he looked aghast at the idea, she added, "I know you scorn town and have vowed never to set foot there; but surely such a vow cannot withstand a sister's urgent need?"

Sir Godfrey sputtered and choked, and seemed with each passing moment to look more defeated and more aged, till Tom Peake took mercy on him and said, "No, I shall go; for my foster-father's long absence from town makes him an ill choice to conduct a search there. The likelihood is that, after a day or so, we would require a second party to search for *him*."

Sir Godfrey must be grateful for this rescue, but seemed less appreciative of Tom's choice of argument.

It was thus agreed that Tom would go.

"And I will accompany him," said Emma.

"Indeed you will not!" said Sir Godfrey. "What service would you provide?"

"You forget, my Aunt Curtis is a woman; and the deep shame she must feel cannot be relieved by anything but another woman's sympathy."

"I am not certain," said Sir Godfrey, "that I would *like* Mrs. Curtis's shame to be relieved. It was honestly come by, after all—if 'honestly' can be the *mot juste* in this context. And besides," he continued, growing red in the face, "if a niece's sympathy were all that was required, why did she flee Frances?"

"Frances is on her honeymoon," said Emma; "a condition compared to which her own is a scandalous mockery. She must look on a bride's regard with horror."

"But not yours?"

Emma blushed. "No, not mine. For I am not in a position either to understand or to judge her. At least, she will think it so. She will persuade herself of it, for her own sake."

Sir Godfrey threw his hands in the air and said, "I will not endeavor further to understand the minds of ladies, whether fallen or otherwise. I might just as profitably undertake to fly by throwing myself off the roof. But if you are so filled with conviction, then let it be so; you may accompany Tom."

Edgar and Emma

On hearing this, Edgar found the determination to do what he had till that moment not quite found the will for. "I shall go as well," he said.

Lady Marlow raised an eyebrow. "You are very generous, Mr. Willmot; but why would you make such an offer?"

"Ralph is my brother; and it is he who has brought Mrs. Curtis to this lamentable state. I therefore see it as my duty to attempt to repair the damage he has wrought. And furthermore," he continued, now addressing Tom, "if we join forces, we will cover twice the ground."

And so it was settled. They would set out for town the very next morning.

Edgar returned to the Lodge and told his mother and sister, who were taking their evening cordials, what been decided. He longed to inform his father, but was told he still would not be disturbed for any thing. "He has taken this greatly to heart," said Mrs. Willmot. "He cannot bear to consider what Mr. Curtis and the Marlows must think of us. It is like a dagger through his heart."

Edgar reassured her that the Marlows were the least censorious people in the world, then went to his room to pack a small valise for what he hoped would be a very short sojourn.

While he was thus occupied, and while Mrs. Willmot poured herself another sherry on the excuse that her nerves demanded it, Patience conceived of a plan; and the more she considered it, the more it excited her. But she must not give voice to it yet; she must wait.

And so she did; she kept her silence all through breakfast the next day, and through Edgar's departure, and even through several subsequent hours, which provided sufficient time for the search party to have long put Marlhurst behind them.

It was only then that Patience spoke.

"Mama," she said, "I have had a thought about Mrs. Curtis. Will she not require clothes, when she is found?"

Mrs. Willmot had to clear away the mists of her own gloom to hear what her daughter was saying. "I beg your pardon, my dear?"

"I speak of Mrs. Curtis," Patience repeated. "She left the village so abruptly; I cannot but think she took little with her—possibly no more than the clothes on her back. Would it not be a great comfort to her, when she is found, to have fresh vestments?"

"I am sure you must be right," said Mrs. Willmot feebly. "I would you had thought of it yesterday."

Patience put down her needlework and met her mother's eyes. "I am glad you agree; but why should one day be any impediment? I propose that I ask Mr. Curtis's permission to choose a few garments from Mrs. Curtis's wardrobe, then deliver them to Edgar, so that he may have them on hand for her."

"What? Oh, no, my dear," said her mother, her shock at the idea restoring vigor to her demeanor. "You, all alone, journeying to town? I cannot approve it, and your father most certainly would not."

"But you have used me for similar errands," Patience protested; "as when I took the charger to Aunt Clayton in Boars Hill."

"Boars Hill is not London, my dear."

"Nor am I helpless, Mama; I am well versed in travel by coach. And when I reach my destination, I will have Edgar's protection. I need only remain long enough to consign to him the clothes I have selected for poor Mrs. Curtis, of whose fate we are not ourselves entirely innocent; for have we both not doted on Ralph, encouraged him in his follies, and diminished his indiscretions?"

These were hard words for Mrs. Willmot to hear; and in order to put a stop to them she agreed to Patience's scheme —with the proviso that Mr. Willmot not be told of it. It was a condition her daughter was very willing to accept.

And so Patience set about realizing her plan—which was exactly as she had explained it to her mother, with two minor variations: wherever she had said "Edgar," she had really meant "Tom;" and when she had said she need only remain long enough to turn over the clothes, she had not added that she might just as easily stay on to help in the search.

CHAPTER TWENTY-FIVE

Mrs. Willmot had a cousin, Mrs. Prothero, who lived on Wimpole Street; the party's plan was to stop first at her house and prevail upon her. This lady had not seen Mrs. Wilmot in nearly forty years, and was thus alarmed at the clutch of earnest, yammering young people who appeared on her doorstep brandishing her name; but soon all was sorted, and Edgar apologized handsomely for arriving in advance of any letter, using the extreme urgency of their errand as his defense.

Mrs. Prothero's husband helped them obtain rooms at a lodging house near Marble Arch; and Emma, while grateful, could not but wonder at this—for she was sure that Marble Arch was not entirely convenient to where Mrs. Curtis had last been seen. Might it not have been preferable to have taken rooms nearer Charing Cross?

It was not until she and Tom and Edgar set out, in the early afternoon, that she understood the reasoning; for Charing Cross was revealed to be a place teeming with persons not entirely respectable. It seemed to her that everyone she encountered had something to sell; and the way in which they insisted that the price was low to the point of madness, very much suggested the opposite. Emma, recoiling, drew closer to Edgar; and he, sensing this, put his arm around her.

Edgar and Emma

And so it was, for Emma, a very strange experience indeed; for she was happy—almost shamefully so, given that it was Christmas week and she was apart from her family, in a thoroughly disreputable part of town, searching out her disgraced aunt. She soon realized that this errand was nigh on impossible; for the streets were a tumult of humanity—beauties and beggars, urchins and usurers, drunkards and dandies, courtesans and costermongers. In all this swarming chaos, it was likelier that Emma would lose her two escorts than that she would locate their quarry.

And yet...she was with Edgar. And when she looked at him now, and saw him with eyes set stonily ahead, his chin held aloft and his stride manly and purposeful, he was restored to the Edgar who had first taken her heart: he who had come up over a rise like the sun at daybreak, plucked her up like Hercules, and carried her home to safety.

She earnestly believed that if anyone could find Mrs. Curtis in this strangulation of people, it was Edgar—and Tom, who was, she now saw, so like Edgar in many ways. Yet they seemed less certain of success; for as the afternoon light faded and dusk drew on, and the lamplighters came out to begin their nightly chore, they agreed that there was no further use in searching; and that on the morrow they would split up, as Tom had suggested the day before at Graftings—which now seemed an age ago and a world away.

They returned to Marble Arch, and were astonished to find Patience awaiting them there, along with a large carrier bag.

"I have brought some clothes for Mrs. Curtis," she said, her eyes darting past them, as though expecting to see that lady follow them in. "Is she not with you?"

221

"We have not yet discovered her, alas," said Edgar. "But how did you know to look for us here?"

"Mrs. Prothero directed me," Patience said with a sidelong glance at Tom, who was himself looking elsewhere.

"You are very good to have thought of Mrs. Curtis's comfort," Edgar said; then he made a helpless gesture at the darkening sky. "It is too late now for you to return to Sussex. I hope that Mr. Prothero has arranged a room for you here, as he has done for us—for between us we have but two."

"I will be happy to share mine, though it will be close quarters," said Emma.

"You are very kind, but it will not be required," said Patience; "Mr. and Mrs. Prothero have offered me their guest room."

"Then let me escort you there forthwith," Edgar said, taking her by the arm and leading her out into the street. As he hailed a cab, Patience looked over her shoulder longingly —as though she were hoping for another to provide the service Edgar had volunteered.

But Tom had already gone upstairs.

The Protheros had just sat down to dinner when Edgar and Patience arrived. Mrs. Prothero asked their nephew to stay, but he excused himself, saying his friends would be waiting to dine with him, and he must not abuse their courtesy.

Then he kissed Patience and said, "I wish you safe travel tomorrow, sister. Christmas Eve! I suppose that will mean the roads are lightly trafficked. Or perhaps it will mean the reverse. Well, when next we meet, you will tell me. Thank you again for your thoughtfulness and for undertaking such an arduous journey; Mrs. Curtis will be deeply grateful. I only pray that we can find her, that she may know of your kindness."

And having said so, Edgar was amazed to see Patience at the lodging house the next morning, when he and Emma and Tom descended for breakfast.

"I thought I might at least contribute to your search," she explained.

Edgar waved away the idea. "It is a very daunting errand we have undertaken; and you have done so much already."

"But I am not easily tired, and I am most observant. I have had so much practice, in my quiet life."

"Your quiet life is precisely at issue," said Edgar, insufficiently disguising his attempt to be genial. "We seek Mrs. Curtis in neighborhoods unsuitable for a country lady."

"And yet Emma accompanies you," Patience protested. "If your protection will do for her"—and here she looked directly at Tom—"why would Mr. Peake's not do for me?"

Tom was startled to hear himself named. "Oh—Miss Willmot! I pray you—do not consider that you might accompany *me*. For I hope today to delve into those districts where no lady may tread without some considerable risk; gentleman escort or no."

"Then why would Mrs. Curtis venture there?" Patience asked desperately.

"Mrs. Curtis would not know better," Tom said with a rueful smile. "Your enthusiasm on my aunt's behalf is very deeply appreciated, I assure you."

"Indeed so," said Edgar; "but you must go home, Patience! It is Christmas Eve. You cannot leave Mama and Papa without your support on such a day as this, when so much is uncertain." Again he took her arm. "We will take you to the coach house and book your passage; and from there we will resume our search."

Patience was by three years Edgar's senior; but he was a man of the world, and she a mere spinster. And when their father was gone, he would be head of the family. She must submit to him; but for the first time in her life, she did not do so with good grace, but turned sulky and incommunicative; not because Edward had offended her, but because Tom Peake had taken so little interest in her that his mind seemed to be entirely elsewhere during all these deliberations.

As they approached the coach house, the trio discussed how best to conduct themselves. "We were entirely too haphazard last night," Edgar said. "We wandered about with no scheme, no strategy. We must be more methodical today."

"I believe it would benefit us to think as my aunt might," said Tom. "We must, to the extent possible, place ourselves in her predicament, and ask, what would we do? Where would we go?"

Edgar booked Patience on a coach headed south, and had instructions drawn out for her on where to change. Again he kissed her goodbye, and Emma did so as well; but Tom Peake merely shook her hand—and looked as though, in his thoughts, he had already left her distantly behind.

As she sat in the coach, awaiting the hour of its departure, Patience reflected on what Tom had said: that in order to discover Mrs. Curtis, they must consider what they, in her place, would do. It was very wise counsel, and Patience was impressed anew with Tom's sagacity, so far beyond that of other gentlemen of his years; what man of forty or even fifty would have the empathy, much less the wisdom, to have come to such a conclusion?

The more she thought on it—and she devoted her whole mind to it, the better to drown out the shrieking of an infant being perhaps too energetically dawdled on its mother's knee in the seat opposite—the more she found herself trying the experiment: were she Mrs. Curtis, and left to her own devices in London, what would she do? Where would she go?

And then she recalled something—a stray comment, made many months before—that caused her heart to trip and skitter; and almost without being fully in command of herself, she rose up from her seat, opened the coach door, and descended; and after being briefly dazzled by the sunlight in her face, she went up to the ticket agent's desk and asked him to direct her to Covent Garden.

Patience was grateful that it was Christmas Eve and not Christmas Day; for the market was still open, and alive with the hum and thrum of commerce.

It had been a good twenty minutes' walk through some neighborhoods Patience hoped she need never traverse again; but once she found herself arrived, surrounded by so much bounty, such a profusion of the world's genius, she was utterly ravished; and the sheer abundance of color and texture, of marvel and delight, very nearly brought her to tears—so small and narrow and grey did her life up to that point seem by comparison.

And when she reached the flower market, she was transported. Everywhere she looked, there were impossible things—blood-red roses by the score (her own beds at home had never yielded more than a scraggly, reluctant clutch of half-barren bushes); summer blooms, brought in from what far-off place she could only imagine; tropical stalks, higher than her head; delicate sprays, so fine she knew not how they could survive human touch.

And there at last, her search came to an end. She came up from behind and touched the familiar shoulder; and when its owner turned in response, she said, "Mrs. Curtis, I beg you do not run from me; I would take you home to those who love you."

Mrs. Curtis was as garrulous as ever on the trek back to Marble Arch; but her speech was disjointed, evidence of a mind seriously shaken.

"You must not think him entirely wicked," she urged Patience, without explaining who "he" was (though there could be no doubt). "He gave me funds to see me home— two pounds! which was very handsome, given that he has not much himself—but I could not bring myself to use them as directed. Go home!—Oh, no; impossible. Home was lost to me forever; and by my own indecent folly. So I sought whatever means I could to live one day after the next—as two pounds will not go far in a city like this, you would be shocked to know how little it will do for you— and I contrived to be hired tying ribbons at the market for Mrs. Vennor; I tie a very pretty ribbon, you will remember —or your mother will, I am certain—but alas! I can never see your mother again—to look her in the face would be death to me. And it is Christmas week, so I was very much needed; so much ribbon—see how my fingers are raw from it! But tomorrow is Christmas Day, and there would be no market, no commerce of any kind, and all of respectable London behind closed doors—and I did not know what I should do—" Here she began to weep. "—How I cursed myself for having fled from Frances! It seemed impossible that anyone else should ever happen upon me—but oh, Miss Willmot! Dearest, gentlest, most ingenious Patience! You are my salvation—you are my deliverer!"

She had not yet exhausted this theme when Tom returned to the lodging house several hours later, bone-tired and bitterly defeated, only to be utterly confounded at finding his aunt there, helping herself to a quantity of biscuits and beer, and singing the praises of her heroine.

"No one so capable as Miss Willmot," she said, gesturing expansively as she did so; "no one more humble and demure, despite her great sense and energy, her uncanny perspicacity and courage. There is none so kind, and none so keen. Oh, my dear Patience! I cannot think of what you have done for me without blushing. Tom, lend me your napkin; I will weep—I know I will weep—"

And as Tom complied, he found himself regarding Miss Willmot with a new appreciation; and to his surprise, he saw much in her that had previously been hidden from him.

At nearly this time, Edgar and Emma—unaware that the object of their search had been safely recovered—continued their forays into the city's more dubious locales. Edgar was nervous of Emma's disposition, but she reassured him that she was entirely without fear.

"I feel safe with you," she said. "Of course I do; for were you not my first rescuer, those many years ago? I cannot imagine that there is anyone with whom I should ever feel safer."

This was so provocative in its artlessness, that Edgar felt he could not mistake its meaning. He must speak. But even now, his habitual uncertainty hobbled his tongue.

"Miss Emma," he said, "I beg your forgiveness if what I have to say offends you. But it appears to me, inexperienced as I am in such things, that you offer me encouragement with regard to obtaining your affections. If this is not your intent—if you merely offer me your friendship, and my own wishes aggrandize this offering into something far greater—you must say so now, that I may be easier in my mind, and not perpetually on the brink of making some unfortunate declaration that will make us awkward with one another."

Her eyes sparkled. "More so than you risk with the declaration you have just made? I cannot imagine what *that* would entail; I might almost wish to hear it." When he blushed up to his cheekbones, she took pity on him and said, "But alas, I must spare you the effort. I *do* mean to encourage you, and I hope that you will take that encouragement to heart; for it is the full extent of my abilities in this matter. As a lady, bound by convention, I may do no more."

And thus an understanding between them was finally achieved; and they continued their search in perfect accord —indeed, with a happiness that was very much at odds with the solemn nature of their mission.

Christmas Day in Marlhurst was less than felicitous for many; but for none more so than Miss Nesmith. By this time, Alice had hoped to be promised—if not actually wed —to Edgar Willmot, and in anticipation of a lifetime of wealth and comfort, and of embracing the wide world and all it had to offer her.

Instead she was more alone than ever, and her world had dwindled to no more than the walls of the parsonage. The hard, unyielding father whose dominion she schemed to escape, had foiled her utterly—by becoming an entirely different man: a broken and needy one. She could not leave him now; it would be monstrous. But she was grateful at least for the daily attendance of Mr. Curtis, who came early and stayed late, and sat with the parson in the interim, so that Alice's interactions with the man who had first created her, then destroyed her, were gratifyingly minimal.

It was late on Christmas Day—after Keppel the cook had gone ahead with the goose purchased earlier in the week for the holiday dinner, despite almost no one being on hand to eat it—that Sir Godfrey Marlow surprised Alice by appearing at the parsonage door. He paid his compliments, and she invited him to share her feast—which she alone enjoyed, seated on a stool and looking idly out the window—but he declined; and Alice was relieved. As wearisome she found her solitary Christmas dinner, it was preferable to the awkwardness that must ensue were she to find herself seated across from the great lord of Graftings, and be forced to make conversation with him.

Sir Godfrey begged leave to speak with Mr. Curtis, and Alice went to fetch him; she found her father's friend spooning broth from a bowl into the parson's trembling lips—a task which Alice was now recruited to take over, so that Mr. Curtis could go out and speak with his brother-in-law.

When they were alone, Sir Godfrey gave Mr. Curtis the news that his wife had been recovered and was quite unharmed. "Even now she is being brought back to Sussex. As she is my sister, I will settle her at Graftings until you have decided where you would have her installed."

Mr. Curtis appeared perplexed. "I thank you, Sir Godfrey, but what is to decide? And why bother with Graftings?

Why may you not simply deliver her to Shakers, which is her home?"

Sir Godfrey's jaw dropped to his chest, almost with an audible thump. "You would have her back?" he gasped.

Mr. Curtis gave him a wry, regretful look. "I understand your incredulity. But I ask you to consider: I took Amelia from your mother when she was but sixteen. You will recall what she was like then: vivacious and charming, but with no experience of the world and no wisdom to guide her through it. As I was her husband—and additionally, a husband so many years her senior—it ought to have fallen to me to provide those things, which your mother surely would have done otherwise. But I failed her. Oh, I made a valiant attempt at the start, but she would not listen; she was too confident in my attraction to care for my opinion. And rather than find a way of making her hear me, I chose to accommodate myself to her deafness. I gave her no instruction, no principles, no rules by which she might improve. And what is worse, I was jealous of my confidences and shared none of them with her, which left her no ally in her own home—no friend to whom she might apply. She must as a result live entirely in her own head, and it was not a well-furnished accommodation." His eyes grew rueful. "I was a lazy husband, brother; I suppose, as an older man, I wanted no more than an ornament as a wife, and I did not care if she were a noisy ornament. And that is exactly what Mrs. Curtis became. She was a creature of endless appetites, with only the veneer of propriety to restrain them. Her sole safety was that in a village such as ours, temptations are few and opportunities for folly scant. Despite which a crisis was inevitable. I gave my wife no counsel, no direction, no intimacy, and no protection. She did not run away; I drove her from me. And yes," he concluded very mildly, "I will be glad to have her back, if she will be so good as to forgive me for it."

CHAPTER TWENTY-SIX

Mr. Nesmith's recuperation was so slow that it was beyond discernment by those who saw him daily; but more irregular visitors spoke of measureable progress. Despite which he remained unable to care for himself, much less perform the duties required of him; and this naturally gave rise to an expectation of replacing him in the Marlhurst living. Mr. Willmot assured Alice that should it come to that, he would provide both a house on the estate for her and her father, and a nurse to look after him; and while she was grateful that she would not be put out to starve, still she knew her situation must be greatly reduced, and she strove to accept it—though her pride and ambition made it a bitter struggle.

Then Mr. Redmond stepped forward and said that he would be happy to move into the parsonage as Mr. Nesmith's caretaker, in the belief that the parson was more afflicted in body than in wit, and that in time he should be sufficiently rehabilitated to resume his offices. Mr. Willmot thanked him, but suggested that there might be some impropriety in a young bachelor living under the same roof as an unmarried girl with an invalid father; a difficulty Mr. Redmond addressed by offering to marry the daughter in question. Alice, who had no other avenue of rescue left to her, agreed; and thus she and her father were able to remain in the parsonage, and the verger became the hero both of his new wife, who was very agreeably surprised by the felicity she found in married life, and of his father-in-law, who did indeed regain most of his strength over the succeeding months. By Easter he was almost his old self again, fulminating from the pulpit that while Christ had risen, it was of no use to any of those assembled before him, for they would surely not follow the Lord to paradise but instead burn to slag and ash in the pit of hell. And so happy were the parishioners to have their firebrand of a pastor restored to them, that they found in this sentence of damnation no small comfort.

As for Patience, she dumbfounded all her friends and family by echoing her mother's epic fecundity, producing seven children over the first six years of her marriage. Tom Peake proved a doting father when he had the chance, but must by necessity dedicate the majority of his waking hours to practicing his profession, as he had a daunting number of mouths to feed.

Mrs. Curtis too enjoyed a long-deferred motherhood; for so complete was her reconciliation with her husband that she was delivered of a son in early autumn, which had the Marlhurst gossips counting back the months in search of scandal; but the calendar was just enough on Mrs. Curtis's side to thwart the effort. She called the boy Horatio after his father, and he became the recipient of all the ardent energy she had previously expended so unwisely, and on objects far less worthy. The Christmas following his birth was thus, for her, the very antithesis of the one before it: she was loved and needed and protected, where she had been abandoned and hopeless and alone. And as she had been forgiven by her husband, and by the village, and had become a doting mother, the recuperated Mr. Nesmith could not inveigh against her without incurring ill will from the community at large, or offending his good friend, her husband; so that she was safe from any mortification from that direction. This might have made her more guarded and circumspect, having so narrowly eluded infamy once; instead she seemed emboldened by her escape, and talked twice as much as before, and three times as carelessly. Drama swirled about her like wind currents for the remainder of her days.

Mr. and Mrs. Denham enjoyed great fame as leading voices in the growing ranks of English dog breeders, and while their British Canine Society never quite became the institution they had hoped, many of its precepts and ideas were adopted by the later founders of the more enduring Kennel Club. Frances had better luck establishing her spaniel dynasty, and for many years Dash and Cannon were highly prized names in a bitch or stud's ancestry.

Violet Cutler married one of the Willmots' tenant farmers and retired from service; her son grew up much beloved of both his mother and stepfather.

Ralph Willmot did indeed discover what is left when one submits to the temptation to smash everything—which is, an utter loss of independence. With no other option left open to him (he had blackened his name in town, and could not return to Marlhurst lest he appall the Curtises) he went to St. Lucia after all, and for two-and-a-half years creditably looked after his father's interests in the sugar corporation, returning a wiser, more seasoned, and more responsible man. Though it soon became apparent that the gravitas he had acquired had been due less to increased sobriety than to lack of opportunity. Once back in England, with its public houses and gaming tables, he returned to form, and was soon in the market for a rich bride, and found one too, so that he was for five or six years very comfortable; until his excesses inevitably reached and then exceeded his new limitations, and his old troubles began anew.

Additionally, he did not depart St. Lucia without leaving a legacy that was, over succeeding generations, to spread its influence far and wide across the island; and that legacy was, the Willmot chin.

And what of our principal hero and heroine? Edgar spent the remainder of his days working on his *Lives of Famous Greeks, Romans and Britons,* with the indispensible aid of his wife. He had nearly finished the work when he died at the age of sixty-three, very little of it having been published. Emma kept his papers in good order, and once her children were grown she devoted herself to editing and annotating them—a task she was yet immersed in when at eighty-one, following a dispute with her eldest daughter-in-law over unequally allotted blueberries at breakfast, she made a great, sulking show of shutting herself up in her room for the rest of her life. Only this time she was as good as her word, as the rest of her life comprised just over four hours.

Edgar's papers were preserved by his descendants, though only because no one could work up sufficient interest to ascertain whether they were worth destroying; and so they languish yet in someone's attic or storehouse, perhaps to be discovered in some unforeseeable future, at which time Edgar Willmot will belatedly become renowned—and his wife too, for being so faithful a sentry to his life's work.

From all of which examples we may conclude that human beings do not change, but remain substantially who we are. We may try to amend our faults, to learn from our mistakes and curb our inclination to repeat the errors in judgment and in conduct that have brought us heartache, or injury, or disrepute; and while the attempt is a noble one, it is never entirely successful. At best, we may sustain such a campaign of improvement for a season or two before succumbing once again to our essential selves, with all their attendant dearths and defects. And when considering the assemblage of personages with whom he has populated this present narrative, and of whom he has grown very fond, your author must confess: he is glad of it.

ABOUT THE AUTHOR

Robert Rodi is the author of ten novels, two memoirs, one story collection, and two volumes of literary criticism; he's also an accomplished monologist and musician. He lives in Chicago with his husband Jeffrey Smith and a constantly shifting number of dogs. For additional information visit his website, www.robertrodi.com

Printed in Great Britain
by Amazon